The Bridge Across the Sky
(and Other Single-Serving Stories)

Chester Tanyeo

The Bridge Across the Sky (and Other Single-Serving Stories)

ISBN (paperback) **978-981-11-0791-7**

First Edition: 8th October 2012

Lunarine Edition: 15th September 2016 (Mid-Autumn)

The Bridge Across the Sky (and Other Single-Serving Stories)

Published by noctalis.com

Singapore

Cake and Vagina

It is a small room. He lies in bed, reading.

The door opens.

One of the girls enter. He looks up as she looks down, her hair a cascading veil, and she holds out a slip of paper.

She had closed the door behind her; stands just beyond the turn of the door, as if she doesn't want to step into the room any more than she already has. He has to get out of bed to pull the slip of paper from fingers slightly trembling.

He sits on the bed, unfolds the note. "I lost a bet." The handwriting is shaky. "I will do whatever you want."

He looks up from this surprise to find her holding her blouse in one hand (the other covering her bra). She glances around the room with a sort of furtive panic, as if looking for a place she could place her blouse without getting it filthy.

His room is clean. The room of one who cleans for a living should be clean, and this one is, but people feel janitors are dirty and so their rooms must be dirty too. He understands this.

His voice is soft: "Put it back on." He gets up, turns his back to her, does something at the table.

A few minutes and he is holding out a mug to her; hot chocolate, wisps of steam curling. "Careful, it's hot."

The eyes which meet his are uncertain and wide with panic. It is obvious she had been crying not long before. But she nods to his smile and reaches out for the drink.

"Wait." He pulls it back. "It's too hot." He places it on the table.

She remains standing. She will have to, he has no seat to offer.

"You can tell your friends we did it, if that helps."

She gives no sign she heard.

"Stay as long as you feel you need to."

Upon the bed, he curls himself with his back towards her.

...

The next morning, he finds the mug, half-emptied. He had forgotten about last night. And he would forget her again, but for now he notes she had switched off the light before she left.

All he remembers is her hair is long and auburn. Sometimes, his eyes would meet one of the girls and he would wonder if it was her.

She is no more than an odd memory when, two weeks after that night, one of the girls casually tosses an empty soda can at a bin as she walks by. The can misses its mark, clutters to the floor. The girl doesn't notice. Nor do the other girls who walk by. It might as well not be there at all.

He is walking towards it when a girl with hair long and auburn lowers herself to pick it up. She hasn't seen him. He stops walking.

Their eyes meet after she commits the can to its destiny.

He nods.

It is a brief moment, but he might have seen a smile as she turns away.

And then she is gone.

That night, his door opens. She enters, carefully closes it behind her. He places his bookmark, looks up.

She stands in the same spot she did before, her hands clasped before her. "Um, hi."

"Hello?"

"I– um. I want to thank you. For that night."

"You're welcome."

He waits for her to leave. Instead, she glances about the room. "Um, I have to do a history paper. I kinda maybe thought I could interview you."

"Okay. We can talk in one of the classrooms."

"No! I mean– we can talk here. If it's okay."

Because you don't want to be seen with me. He feels stupid for suggesting it. "I'm sorry there's no chair. I'll go get one from a classroom."

"No!" She looks around. Then she lowers herself to the floor, seats herself cross-legged. She takes out a notepad from her bag. "It's about World War Two."

"Oh. How old do you think I am?"

"I'm sorry! I kinda thought– I don't know what I thought! I–"

She looks like a frightened kitten. He softens. "I could help. If you don't need an interview. I've read some."

"That would be great. Thank you."

"What's it about?"

"Um, why it happened."

"I see. It happened because if you push countries down too much for too long, they push back."

"Like people."

"Exactly like people."

There is a pause and he realises she's waiting. So he talks. Slowly at first, but then the memories peek out and follow one after the other, and he is just talking: not only about the causes but about the war itself, about the reconstruction after, talking to her earnest eyes and her emotive face, neither of them noticing as the notebook leaves her hand to sit forgotten on the floor. She drinks hot chocolate and she stretches out her legs. He drinks hot chocolate and he tries not to notice those legs.

Then he says: "What time is it?"

She looks at her watch. "Oh my God!"

And then she is gone.

Days later, she enters and she smiles. "I got an A! Thank you!"

"Congratulations." He smiles. In the face of that sunshine, how could he not?

"Do you know as much about the First World War?"

"I know some."

"Could you tell me? Um. Lemme check." She sits upon the floor and she stretches her legs and she smooths out the plaid of her skirt. She pulls out her notebook. "What caused it to end? Was there anything like the bombs? Little Boy and Fat Man," she looks up and smiles. "I remember."

"You did," he laughs. "Well, firstly, it was called the 'Great War'. Nobody called it the First World War until the sequel..."

The night after, she enters and drops her bag on the floor and heads for his table.

She hasn't spoken and he curiously watches her back. She makes hot chocolate, then she turns around and hands him a little paper plate with a slice of cake.

She sits down on the bed, next to him, grinning. She is amazingly pretty when she smiles; the kind of pretty a janitor of a school full of pretty girls does not see every day, does not see at all.

She sticks her fork into her own cake. "Tell me stuff."

"What about?"

"Anything. World War Two."

"Okay. Have I told you about the White Death?"

He talks. She listens. They eat. Empty plates join mugs of chocolate – full, half-full, empty – on the aged wood of the table.

Then he tells her about the Liberation of Paris. "They pulled these women into the streets, women who were said to have slept with the Germans, they called it 'collaboration horizontal'. Publicly, they shaved their heads. One woman, surrounded by a laughing crowd, having her head shaved."

"They cut their hair?"

"They did, yeah."

She doesn't reply and he looks up; her face is blank. He waits a moment. She doesn't say anything, so he fills the silence with the only thing he has to fill it with, facts: "There was this thing in the news recently. This father told his daughter not to do something and she did it. So he cut off her hair and posted the video on the Internet. She killed herself."

"Yeah, I know. She's four years younger than me."

"It's not just the cutting of her hair, it's the publicness of it. The public shaming, like when we used to put people in stocks in the public square. It's as if by removing her femininity you destroy the woman herself. And it sort of doesn't make sense, because, I mean... They remove something which makes a woman attractive, but a woman should be more than how attractive she is, she should be more than her hair, her worth should be more than being attractive, and, moreso, attractive to men. If you destroy her hair it shouldn't be destroying the only thing about her which matters. Women should be more than that."

She smiles, shakes her head in a way more herself. "You have no idea what it's like to be a woman."

"I suppose not."

"Okay, it's kinda true. Women should be more than that, but we live in a world where a woman could be running for president and what they'll talk about is her hair."

"Yes."

"Tell me something else. I don't want to hear about that anymore."

He tells her about the places during the war which saw no combat but were very much a part of the war nonetheless. Wars used to be like that, you didn't have to be in uniform to know a war was being fought. It's not that way anymore, wars are more distant now. People don't notice anymore. They talk about other things. They talk about hair.

The night after, she boils the water and she sits down upon his bed and she removes her shoes. She stands, shoes in hand, looks around. "Where are your shoes?"

"Under the bed."

"Oh." She places her shoes, makes hot chocolate. She climbs onto his bed, curls her legs in and hugs them, rests her chin upon her knees. She grins. "Do you know anything about Sumeria?"

"Sumeria?"

"Before Babylon, there was Sumeria."

"Ah. That Sumeria. I know some."

She looks at her palm. "Early Mesopotamia. Tigris, Euphrates. Sumeria, Akkadia, Babylonia, Assyria."

He stares at her for a moment. "How old are you?"

"Seventeen."

"And they're teaching you this?"

"They are."

"It doesn't seem very useful."

"It's kinda not. Actually, they're two separate classes. Modern and ancient history. Bores me to tears. Except the way you tell it. You talk as if you were actually there."

"What's your paper on?"

"Anything at all. We're allowed to focus on whatever we want."

"Mankind's earliest achievements came from then; writing, a legal system. It was the birth – well, *a* birth – of civilisation. And of course Nebuchadnezzar is in the Bible."

"Say that again."

"Nebuchadnezzar."

"You're not making this up, are you? Because that sounds like two bad words said together."

"Of course I'm not."

"Okay. Tell me about him."

He talks. She listens. He wonders if she knows, the way she's sitting, he can see her underwear. She probably doesn't. The girls sit that way all the time, during lunch, scattered around school, clustered in small groups. It is a girl's school, and they feel safe and comfortable and nobody is watching.

He doesn't look during the day, and he doesn't look now.

Except that, right now, he is very conscious he isn't looking.

She comes for two more nights. She brings cake on the last.

Her delight overflows on finding out Woodrow Wilson's best friend is named Colonel House. "That's like the show! House and Wilson."

"What show?"

"It's not important." She smiles.

She seems to smile a lot.

The weekend comes and he looks up at every sound. But the door never opens.

No girl enters.

She comes back on Monday and Tuesday and Wednesday.

On Thursday –

She enters. She brings cake. She smiles.

After she settles – seated cross-legged opposite him on the bed, the paper plate in her lap – he says: "Are you okay?"

"How do you know?"

"I don't know. It's just... you don't seem okay."

Her head already bowed, she turns aside; looking away even though she wasn't looking at him to begin with.

He puts his plate on the table. "Do you want to talk about it?"

She doesn't look up. She shakes her head.

"Is there anything you want me to tell you about?"

She shakes her head.

"I could tell you about the Merovingians."

She doesn't react.

"The Merovingians, the *Mero*vingians, the Merovin*gians*! Now that's an interesting story."

No response.

"They were the people who ruled France before it was France, before it was Gaul." Long pause. "That's all I know."

There is silence for a long moment. Then she kicks him.

"Can you at least smile?"

She looks up, smiles, but it doesn't reach her eyes. The silence descends, slowly, as her head gently bows.

He tries to think of something to say. Some story to make her smile. He had never thought of history as exciting but she seems to be excited, swept up by... he doesn't know by what. But history isn't funny. History doesn't make anyone smile. It is about the opposite of humour, it is the long dark road we walked to reach where we are now. History is about a time when there was less freedom and more unfairness.

She says: "That first night."

She's looking down at her hands, holding the edges of the paper plate and turning it around and around, slowly, like a makeshift rosary.

Her voice comes in a soft whisper, wafting upon the silence: "There's this guy. I met him at a party. He's really nice and… um– Long story short, I went to his house one night and we had sex. He has a girlfriend but he said it was over. I… except– um– except it *wasn't* over. The girlfriend and her friends… I had to come in here and– or they would cut off my hair. Then they had their revenge and it was fine. I guess. For a while. And– but– and I came back. You were so nice, so I came back, to thank you. But when I was here I saw your," she waves at his stacks of books, "I don't know why I didn't just leave, I kinda asked you about World War II and… and yeah."

"It's okay."

She shakes her head. "It's not okay. It's not okay at all." She waves at the cake box. "They know I come here after school. I wait in the library but someone always sees. The school is never empty. They know how late I stay. They know I bring you cake. It's not something I can hide."

"You should stop coming then."

She is silent for very long. He watches, helpless, as a tear falls onto her cake. Her hands move. "You don't understand."

The silence stretches.

He says: "Guys are always nice, you know. If they want to sleep with you. It doesn't mean they're honest, it doesn't mean they're sincere. It doesn't even mean they're nice. It just means they want something. People who want something are always nice."

Silence.

"You should stop coming."

She slowly shifts her feet to the floor, places the plate upon the table, slouches forwards like a puppet whose part in the play is over. "They gave out my number. I've been receiving texts all day. If you sleep with the janitor you must sleep with anyone, right?"

He wants to fix this. Of course he wants to fix this. He's angry. And he's... sad. Sad because she's sad. Sad because he can't fix this; he doesn't know how.

He says, at last: "Don't come back anymore." It's the only answer he has.

She wipes her eyes with the back of her hand. She doesn't look at him. "You don't understand at all." She puts on her shoes.

He watches. He watches, helpless, as she just sits there. He watches, useless, as she pulls her bag to her, as she rummages within and as she stands up.

She doesn't turn. There is a note in her fingers, stretched out behind her. He reaches out to take it.

And then she is gone.

The note says: "I don't care what they say. I just wanted to tell my only friend."

How is he supposed to make this right?

He wants to go to the administration but how is he even going to begin? How do you tell someone you're *not* sleeping with a student?

Sometimes he sees her turn around and away. She's avoiding him. But even if she isn't, even if he could go up to her... he can't talk to her in public. That'd only make it worse.

He has to clean the graffiti in the washrooms. Too many of them bear her name. It's wrong, it's so wrong he now knows her last name and her phone number. That she hasn't told him, that he finds out in this way. He doesn't keep her number. He keeps scrubbing, as if cleaning away the words can clean as well his soul.

Too many of them bear her name.

Or Friday, she enters and she places a cake box on his table.

And then she is gone.

There is a note in the box. It says: "i miss you." The "i" is dotted with a heart.

Into the silence, he says: "I miss you too."

It is a silence which isn't silence, because the radio is playing.

But it still feels like silence.

Something which is there, but isn't heard, but isn't seen. It might as well not be there at all.

He has to let her know. But he doesn't know how. It is all he thinks about.

Monday comes and he tries to find her at lunch. But the school is a big place and there are many girls with hair long and auburn.

He feels stupid for not keeping her number. But she probably already changed it.

And even if he could get her a message, what would it say?

I miss you. Come back.

What good would that do?

A message which can't be sent.

On Monday night, she enters and he sits up at once and he catches hold of her wrist. "Don't go."

"I can't stay."

"Then why come at all?"

"I can't not."

"How are you hiding the cake box?"

"I'm not."

"So they know."

"They know I'm sleeping with you."

"But that's not true!"

"It doesn't have to be. Let go please, you're hurting me."

Surprised, he releases his grip.

She is already at the door when he says: "Stay!"

She doesn't turn. She stands, hand on the knob, as if she is about to say something. But nothing is said.

And then she is gone.

He can't find her during lunch. He tries. He fails.

The next day, she enters and drops the cake box on the table and turns to leave.

Into the blur of her motion, he says: "If I disappeared–"

She stops at the door.

"If I disappeared, someone else would take this job. No one in this world would notice I was gone. As long as the trash cans are emptied and the floors are mopped, no one notices I'm here. No one notices me. You're the only person I matter to. You make me matter. So I'm sorry. I'm sorry and I miss you."

She stands, her back towards him, for a very long moment.

She turns. "You can't say things like that. I'm supposed to be angry with you."

"I'm sorry."

"Yeah fine." She sits on the bed, removes her shoes.

He watches, uncertain, as she settles.

Then she smiles at him, bright and honest. She brings her knees up to her chin. "Tell me stuff."

And, just like that, it is as if everything is normal again. Except there is only one slice of cake.

But that's okay.

Because she's here to share it with him.

The next day, he goes to find her during lunch. He had asked her where she disappears to.

She sits in a quiet spot behind one of the buildings, eating a sandwich and reading a book.

He keeps his distance, clearing the leaves from the drains.

She spots him, smiles. He smiles back.

Then her head drops as she looks back at her book. She brushes her hair behind her ear. She doesn't stop smiling.

She's there every night. Sometimes she brings cake.

"I'm going to have a perfect attendance this term," she says, after she stops coughing, "because of you."

He's always there, during lunch. He always keeps his distance.

Even though there is never anyone around, he never talks to her. Not during the day, when they are different people because the world is a different place.

She smiles to herself as she reads.

He finishes his work day and returns to his room to find her on his bed, reading.

It's early, far earlier than she usually comes.

She sits up. "I'm not going to hide in the library anymore. Gossip only has power if you care what it says, and I'm not going to care anymore."

"Are you sure?"

She shrugs. "Yeah, why not? I'm already that girl. It's old news now anyway. I might as well stop letting it inconvenience me."

"I suppose that makes sense."

"Good."

"But what if those girls– you know."

"What would you do?"

"Me? Stand up to them. Make them stop."

"Then that's what I'll do. I'll make them stop. And from now on I'll be coming here straight after class, so you can have my delightful company for a few more hours."

He smiles. "I'd like that."

She says: "You're nice."

"Thank you."

"You told me guys are nice if they want to have sex with you."

"I did. It's not always true but it's true enough."

"Why have you never tried to? Have sex with me."

Apropos of nothing. "I– It's not right."

She tilts her head, smiling playfully. "Do you think I'm ugly?"

"Of course not."

"Are my boobs too small?"

"No, it's not that. I would lose my job."

She laughs. "Liar."

"What?"

"I've been coming here for... since term started. Three months now. The whole school thinks we're sleeping together."

"Yes, but it's not true." The weight of his embarrassment forces his gaze downwards, away from her sparkling eyes.

"It doesn't have to be. What I mean is, you kinda still have your job."

"It's not that simple."

"But it is though. You either find me attractive or you don't. It's what all men want, isn't it? Sex?"

"That's not always true."

"It doesn't have to be. It just has to be true for you."

"I'm gay."

"Liar."

"Oh stop accusing me. How would you know if I'm gay or not?"

She doesn't reply. She's doing something; he looks up to find her pulling her underwear along her legs. At once, he shifts his gaze to her eyes; they stare unflinchingly back. He turns away. She tosses her underwear onto his lap.

After a moment of indecision, he carefully picks them up and holds them out to her. She doesn't take them back.

"If you're gay... look. It won't turn you on."

"What's come over you?" He releases her underwear, withdraws his arm.

"I'm kinda curious."

"I think you should leave."

"No."

They sit in a silence he finds incredibly awkward. He doesn't know how she feels about it because he doesn't dare look at her.

At last, he says: "This isn't like you."

"How would you know?"

"I–"

"You think you know me but you don't. So how'd you know?"

"I do know you. Not all of you, but I–"

"You see someone who isn't me, you don't see me at all. That guy, that lying bastard. I went to his house expecting to have sex. He wasn't my first."

"That's not the point."

"Do you prefer if I was a virgin?"

"No, of course not. That's not what I mean… I don't even know what I mean."

"I could be a whore. I could be a virgin. Not like either of those things reflect who a person is. And you wouldn't know."

There's movement.

And then she is gone.

Her underwear is still on his bed. He sits there, not exactly sure what had happened, then he picks them up and pulls open a drawer.

Stuck to the wall, there is a note. "Think about this."

It is as if last night never happened. They talk as they always talk. There is cake.

Then, with stunning suddenness, she is pulling down her underwear and he is flush with embarrassment.

She says: "I'm a whore. Those cakes you eat. I pay for them by opening my legs."

"But– That's not true."

She sighs theatrically. "Every weekend, I meet a stranger and he pays me for sex. Some of them are younger than you are, young and handsome and you wonder why they even have to pay. But they do. Some are old, fat, kinda gross, I guess, but I have sex with them too–"

"No. But... you're so shy. That... first night you came here."

"I was shaken. I had just been threatened."

He remembers. He calls up the image easily. Her arm is covering her bra as she looks for a place to put her blouse. Covering her bra. That's not something a prostitute would do. A prostitute wouldn't call herself a 'whore' either. "No. You're too shy."

"They like that I'm shy. They like that I turn away when they try and kiss me. They find it amusing. When I push their hands away from my breasts they move my hands over my head. They hold my hands with one hand and they grab my breasts with the other. I always wonder if they notice how lightly their hand is placed on my wrist, how easy it is to hold me down, but I don't think they–"

"Stop it. Okay. I believe you."

"You don't like hearing about me having sex? Or are you just pretending not to like it? Do you want to know what they like best?"

"Just stop."

"More than one guy told me this: They like that I turn my face away before they put it inside me but then I cry out for more." She moans.

He stands up.

On his way out, his leg bumps against her foot, dangling off the bed because she had opened her legs.

The room is empty when he returns. Her underwear is gone. There is a note on the wall, stuck next to the first: "Sorry."

He says: "If you remove your underwear again, I'm leaving."

It is a nice, normal night. With cake.

It is another nice, normal night until he notices she isn't wearing underwear.

He looks away at once. He turns back to find her smiling at him, as if daring him to say something. Her smile is both playful and slightly cruel, like the smile of a cat if cats could smile.

The realisation hits him with all the force of an epiphany: All those nights with her sitting with her knees pulled up, *of course* she knew she was exposing herself. She'd have to be stupid or innocent not to know. She's not stupid, not stupid at all. She's so not stupid she can't be innocent. More than that, he knows this: He wants to think her innocent but, deep down, he knows it isn't true. Youth and innocence may come together, but how she looks isn't who she is.

After a moment, he says to her mischievous eyes: "What were we talking about?"

"I forgot."

He wants to pretend normality but... but he just *can't*. "Why are you so intent on this?"

"On what?"

"Isn't it enough I want to?"

"No, it kinda isn't."

"I'm too old for you."

"I kinda don't care."

"I'm just a janitor."

"I kinda already know that."

"No you don't. You don't understand. You have a bright future ahead of you. And... and I'm just a janitor."

"My future?" Her smile fades. "Oh." Her eyebrows knit, then relaxes. "You thought about it. You thought about... being with me. Like, as a couple."

"I don't have to think about it. It's obvious. It's the very first thought. I'm a janitor and–"

"No." She shakes her head. "You have no idea what guys would give to fuck me. I'm offering you just that, and you don't want it because what you care about is my future?"

"I guess so."

"This is my day."

"What?"

"This is my day. This is the only part of the day which matters to me. I think about the stories you tell so I can ask questions so I have something to say. I think about what cakes we haven't tried. I think about..." She shakes her head. "I have no friends here. I'm like a damn leper in this messed up school, one of those poor people you told me about, invisible yet avoided. But, you know, I don't care about that. I'm invisible but I still hear stories. I still see the girls crying in the washrooms. I'm not the only one messed up by this place. And that guy? You know... I didn't go there expecting to sleep with him. He told me there were other people there, we were going to hang out. But then it was only him. I let him kiss me. I kissed him back. I let him touch my breasts. Then I realised how much I didn't like him. Then I realised I kinda didn't like myself more. He had lied to me and then I had gone and... agh.

"Fuck him. They're like that. Of course they're not all like that but so many of them are. They're nice. Nice guys who want something. But one night I had no choice but to give myself to a stranger and... he didn't want me. I would have been raped. I was so afraid. They had scissors in their hands and they were so angry with me. I didn't even do what they said I did. I was so scared and I thought they were going to do so much worse than cut my hair. I was so afraid I was almost grateful when they said they'd let me go if I fucked the janitor. I came in here because it was away from them. I would have been raped, I would have let myself be raped. If it had been anyone else but you."

Quiet.

He says: "You don't owe me anything."

Her anger, he is learning, is sudden and unpredictable. "You think I'm *paying a debt*?!"

She has put on her shoes and reached the door when she turns around. She stomps back to him. "Look at me," she hisses.

He does.

She punches him in the shoulder.

And then she is gone.

During lunch, he waits for her at her usual spot but she doesn't show. She doesn't come to his room.

The day passes.

Then the days after pass too.

He is walking to the nurse when she appears beside him.

Without a word, she walks with him. He can feel the eyes all looking, looking, looking. He knows they're not just looking at his hand, however bloody it is.

…

The nurse says: "Go to class."

She looks at the nurse and she looks at him and her eyes brim with concern.

He smiles. "It's just a small cut. It looks worse than it is."

The nurse nods. "He'll be fine."

…

The nurse's eyes never leave the bandage her hands slowly wrap around his wound. "Do you know anything about the expelled girls?"

"I know three of them got expelled. I don't know anything else." It's been a few days and the whole school is still talking about it.

"Do you know who they are? The queen bee and her friends." There's a sort of excitement in the way she said it.

He doesn't care but he doesn't have the heart to stop her. "You must hear all the latest. I don't even know why they got expelled."

"Apparently, this pimp got arrested for having underaged girls and those three are his… well, they were on his payroll. They don't just expel someone for anything, no. The *police* are involved." She pauses a moment for this to sink in. "Now our royal majesty claims she was framed."

"Claims she was framed?" One can appear interested by just repeating the last point as a question.

"Oh yes! I believe her. I don't see her as needing the money. I think she pissed off the wrong girl and they put her number into the pimp's phone."

"But how would they even be able to do that?"

"Speculating, don't quote me. They pretended to be her online and gave him her number. I'm sure pimps are always on the lookout for more staff."

"HR must be a nightmare. But they'd have to find a pimp first, and then pretend to be someone else, and then turn the pimp in. That seems too elaborate."

"You think so?"

"People don't plan so much. People don't plot. It's more likely they already knew him, and when they wanted revenge, they saw their chance and they took it."

"Yeah, that does make more sense." She finishes with the bandage, gives it a pat. "There."

...

She is standing in the empty hall, leaning against the wall.

He shows her the bandage.

She nods. "Good."

"I'm sorry. Please stop being angry. I'm wounded."

"That had nothing to do with me."

"Yeah, but I'm in pain. You can't be angry at someone in pain."

"So I have to stop being angry because you hurt yourself?"

"That's the way the world works."

She glares, twists her mouth. "Fine. I'll come by later."

"Thank you." He feels stupid as soon as he says it.

"Yeah. I have to get to class."

That night, she sits down opposite him and she pulls his hand to her and she looks at the bandage.

"I'm fine."

She nods, but she doesn't let go. Instead, she tilts herself forwards until the top of her head is against his shoulder, his hand closed in both of hers.

The silence feels warm.

She says, softly. "You're wrong."

She pulls herself back, looks him in the eyes. "You're wrong. I have a bright future but that doesn't mean I can't have it with you. And *that* doesn't mean I want to get married right away either. But you keep saying you're just a janitor and you think that's a bad thing but when I go off to uni it means you can come along. So maybe I kinda maybe thought about it too. But that's two years away and anyway we kinda don't know if we'll still be together then. Seeing as you can be a jerk."

"I see," he says, not entirely sure he does. Just in case, he says: "I'm sorry."

"I hate this school and the only thing I think about on the weekends is coming back here. I don't have a lot of experience with this sort of thing but I'm pretty sure that means we're not just friends."

"Okay."

"Okay."

"Okay."

"So I have a paper on the Crusades."

The next day, at lunch. She sits upon the raised concrete and she reads. He sweeps the fallen leaves.

After a few minutes, her eyes never leaving her book, her legs slowly open.

After ten minutes, she puts her book aside. She removes her shoes.

She glances around. There is no one about, there never is.

She looks directly at him, holding his gaze and smiling her smile and she slides her underwear down along her legs.

She places it on her book, as if it's the most normal thing, and she puts on her shoes.

He stands still as she walks towards him.

As if it's the most normal thing, she drops the white on the pile of leaves as she walks by.

He says: "The three girls who got expelled, were they the...?"

"How do you know?"

"I don't."

"They were. Miserable bitches."

"The nurse said she claimed she was framed. Said someone pretended to be her online and gave him her number, and that's why her number is in his phone. It just doesn't seem likely to me. People don't plot revenge. It's always a spur of the moment thing."

"I think people do plot. Perhaps not as much as pretending to be someone else online, but they could think about the easiest way to get their revenge. If she was framed."

"How would they do it? Say you knew a pimp, you can't just put a number into their phone. They'd notice. And if you did know a pimp, that would make him a friend and you wouldn't turn him in."

"He doesn't have to be a friend. He could be her pimp. When he's washing up after sex, there's enough time alone with his phone."

"No, no. Pimps don't have sex with their girls. It's a common misconception."

"Maybe not all of them. I'm sure some pimps take their commission with sex in addition to cash."

He nods. "But that'd imply one of the girls here is a prostitute."

"You have no idea. We all wear the same uniform but have you seen their bags? Some girls are carrying bags worth thousands of dollars. I'll be surprised if none of them were."

"Well, I can tell your bag isn't worth thousands of dollars."

"If I were a prostitute, I wouldn't spend the money on bags."

"What would you do with it, the money?"

"Keep it."

"I see."

"Yup."

"Hmm. Did you have anything to do with getting them expelled?"

"How could I?"

He doesn't know what she means. Was it "How could I do such a thing?"; that she's incapable of an act so morally dubious? Or was it the literal "how"; the practical steps to commit such an act? Perhaps it's best not to ask. Perhaps it's best not to know. "Yeah, of course you couldn't. I don't even know why I asked."

"If she's innocent, if she was framed... I kinda don't care. She deserved it."

He nods. He can't quite agree with the morality but he can't deny the– the justice in this. "She does."

"If you push people too far, they push back."

"They do."

"How do you know so much about history?"

"There's a good library here. Janitors don't get paid enough I can afford other entertainment."

"Then why are you a janitor?"

"There aren't a lot of jobs for..."

"For?"

"People like me."

She crosses the bed, settling herself with her legs folded beneath her. She pulls his hand into hers, runs her fingers carefully over the tattoo on the underside of his forearm: a stylised hourglass. "The other girls, they say you were in prison."

"No."

"If you were, would you tell me?"

"Since you asked."

She shakes her head. "You shouldn't. I wouldn't, if I were you. I'd lie."

"You shouldn't lie."

She shrugs. "No one should. But people do anyway." She closes her hands over his. "I don't want to know. I imagine you were in prison, or a soldier, or in a gang. I imagine you were in a hard place, but instead of making you hard, it made you soft. I don't want to know it's something you did one drunken night with your friends, or you got it for an ex-girlfriend. I know the truth of you, on the inside. The man I know is soft, who offers hot chocolate to a girl who is offering him... something else." She smiles, a little wistful. "Lies are always beautiful, because you get to choose them. Your lies are your own. Truth is... Truth is painful. Truth belongs to other people."

"Like putting on a mask. Inside truth and outside lie. Or even wearing make-up."

"I didn't expect you to agree."

"I don't agree, but I do understand."

"The truth of a person isn't in what they've done, it's in what they do. Who you were isn't who you are. I know the man I see. Your past doesn't matter to me, so it might as well be beautiful. You can be the person I want you to be, and I can be the person you imagine me to be. I might wear make-up for you. I might make myself beautiful for you."

"You're already beautiful. You're always beautiful."

She smiles. "When you see me in make-up, you'll know you just told a lie."

At lunch, she slowly opens her legs.

She doesn't slide her underwear down. She isn't wearing any.

She is removing her shoes when he says: "You have to stop doing this."

"Doing what?"

"You know what. Sex isn't... it isn't a game. It's something precious. Between people who love each other."

Still bent over, she turns her head to focus her glaring eyes upon him.

She stands up.

He notices her shoes are back on. "What did I say?"

She ignores his protestations.

She takes the cake with her.

...

She comes back five minutes later.

She stares at him, hands on hips, the cake box clenched by a fist, tilted at an angle obviously unfavourable to the structural integrity of baked goods.

He says: "The cake box is tilted at an angle obviously unfavourable—"

She raises a finger.

In a panic, he says what he feels is becoming a new default: "I'm sorry."

"What for?"

"For saying what I said."

She nods. "Don't say such things again."

"I won't." He still hasn't figured out what he had said wrongly. He can't quite figure out how to get the answer from her. Perhaps he should just give up on getting her to give up. But... he can't do that. At this rate, he's bound to give in. He's barely holding on as it is. He feels the weight of resisting the stereotype of his entire gender bearing down: "Cake and vagina. Who says 'no' to that?"

The owner of both is, right now, annoyed at him. "The cake is ruined. It's all your fault."

He takes the plate she offers. The cake is in slightly better shape than he had expected. "I'm sorry. It becomes mush in your stomach anyway."

"That really hurt."

"I'm sorry."

"I can't believe you said that."

"I'm sorry."

"Promise me you won't say it again."

Oh dear.

The pause must have been too long because she pulls the plate from his hands. "You don't know!"

"I–"

"For fuck's sake!"

"Calm down."

"Don't tell me to–! Agh. I *know* you don't love me, okay? You don't have to tell it to my face like that!"

"I never said I didn't..."

"*Do* you?"

"I–"

She holds the plate up, showing him the crumbled cake. She moves it left and right, as if testing his visual acuity. Then she tips the plate into the bin.

...

He looks at the closed door and he sighs. "I don't have to take this kind of emotional abuse from a woman I'm not sleeping with."

And the problem with that is this: It is too easy to balance that equation.

Either he got better at apologising or she's getting used to it.

The next day is normal, and the day after that.

She visits on a Saturday night. She's wearing lipstick.

He says: "It's Saturday." It sounds stupid.

"I kinda know that."

"You do look good with make-up."

"I kinda know that too. And you're not allowed to judge me."

"Huh? Judge you why?"

"Because you think a woman should be more than how attractive she is to men."

"There's nothing wrong with wanting to be attractive. The point is it has to be your choice, not a choice made for you."

"Well, it's my choice. I do think a woman should be more than how attractive she is to men, but I think it's okay if she wants to be attractive for one man, not all of them."

"I... I suppose that is okay."

"Good. I'm glad we agree. Also, I'd like it if we could have lunch together. The furtive glances thing was sweet for a while, but now, not so much."

He can think of so many reasons not to. He hears himself say: "Yeah. Let's do that."

...

Before she leaves, she stands at the door and says: "When term break comes, I've decided to visit my brother at uni. Six whole weeks. I'll probably meet a guy. We might fall in love. We'll have sex. I'll tell you all about it when I come back. That's okay, because we're just friends."

And then she is gone.

She says: "Are you seeing anyone?"

"Eh?"

"It's a simple question."

"No."

"I kinda wanted to be sure. I don't know what you do on the weekends."

"I read."

"I know. You said. But– Nevermind. Is it because I'm seventeen?"

"No."

"I'm legal. I kinda checked. Just for you."

"It's not because you're seventeen."

"You know what's funny about being seventeen though? Looking at my parents, work is kinda your entire life. It's like, oh, 75% of your waking hours, and the rest is the going there and coming back and eating and the... the maintenance. The keeping yourself alive. So you are able to work.

"My parents have these dinner parties, and mother would say 'That's so-and-so, she's a banker.' Or a lawyer or something. As if that's the most important thing about the person, their defining characteristic. What they do isn't just what they do, it's kinda what they are. As if, deep down, they have the heart of a banker or the soul of a lawyer.

"They become invisible. Who they are is no longer relevant beneath what they do. They become no more than their function. What makes a lawyer any different from any other lawyer? A banker from any other banker?

"What I'm studying, here and now, it'll decide what I get to study in uni, which will decide what I'm qualified to do for the rest of my life. And seventeen year olds are asked to decide – we're told to decide – to make this decision about the rest of our lives, this future set in motion. We have to do this and yet we cannot be trusted to choose who we love and what we want to do with them? I know teenagers do dumb things. But that doesn't mean we only do dumb things. That we can't make the right decisions sometimes."

"You're right."

"Yeah, well. Anyway, tell me about Yamamoto."

"I thought you covered World War Two?"

"You said it was an assassination. I'm curious about that."

...

Before she leaves, she plants her feet in front of him and lifts up her skirt. "Just look. This look away thing of yours was cute in the beginning but it kinda got old. So just look. It's not as if you haven't been looking all night. And for weeks."

He doesn't look.

"I shaved. I was wondering if you prefer if I didn't?"

"..."

"It's a simple question. A yes or no will do."

"No."

"No, I shouldn't shave? Or no, I should stop? And, yes, I realise now it's not a yes or no question."

"No, don't stop."

"We're kinda a couple. You're not seeing anyone and I'm not seeing anyone and it's obvious we're not just friends. You think it's wrong to sleep with me but just ask yourself what you're doing now. I can't date anyone else. I'm yours. Whether or not you choose to admit it, I'm yours. Whether or not you do anything with me, I'm not able to do that with someone else. I can't. I don't want to. So what you're doing, that's wrong too. You're leading me on. You don't have to decide now, but at some point you have to choose to break my heart or sleep with me."

"..."

"Once, a few weeks ago, I stayed outside your door because I didn't want to leave. I heard you lock it. Every night since, a minute after I leave, I hear the lock click. I imagine you jerk off. It gets me wet. I'm so wet right now I can feel it."

He looks. Only for a split-second, before his guilty eyes flick to hers.

She's grinning. "Don't stop now. It's too late for pretense."

He watches as she reaches between her legs. She *is* wet. He doesn't realise his mouth is open until she dabs the salt on his lower lip. She releases her skirt.

She sticks a note on the wall.

And then she is gone.

The note says: "Waiting."

He says: "I just got paid. I should give you some money, for all the cakes."

"I don't want your money."

"I'm not giving you money, I'm paying for my share."

She reaches out for her bag, pulls out a handful of crumpled currency. "This is how much my parents love me."

"Even so, you shouldn't."

"Shouldn't *what*? Show I care by buying you cakes? Money is love. My parents love me, so they give me money. I buy you cakes."

"Money isn't love."

"Ha!" Her face is mean. "This from the man who can't love me because he is a janitor and janitors are *poor*."

"It's not like that."

"Isn't it though? I don't look down on you but it doesn't matter to you because you look down on yourself."

"It's not like that."

"Of course it's not. What is love, then? Sex? Because you don't want that from me either."

He is quiet. She holds his gaze for a while before she looks down.

In the silence, she sniffles.

He says, softly: "I like today's cake."

She nods to the crumpled notes in her hands.

"I'm sorry."

She nods.

"I like those with a cherry on top."

"I'll give you my cherry."

"You don't have to."

She shakes her head. She slowly looks up and she smiles slightly. "You were kinda doing so well."

"Eh?"

"Try again."

"Oh. I like cake with a cherry on top."

"I'll give you my cherry."

"I– I'd like that."

She smiles. "See? That wasn't difficult."

...

Before she leaves, she says: "I don't have to go on holiday, if I have a reason to stay."

And then she is gone.

"I'm thinking of maybe taking history at uni. But my parents want me to take something practical."

"They're right."

"You think so? You know all this history and you can't make a cent from it. I noticed something. Bankers and lawyers and doctors, they have degrees you can make money from. And then there are degrees you can't make money from. These degrees which can't make money don't have people. A law degree makes you a lawyer and a medicine degree makes you a doctor. But literature and history, nobody is defined by them. And those degrees you can't make money from, we call them the humanities. We call them that because it's the stuff of what makes us human. And yet it can't buy you stuff. It's like nobody cares what's in our head, what's in our soul. It scares me. I'm scared if I take something practical, I'll become someone who stops caring, I'll become my degree."

"There are historians."

"Oh yeah! But you get my point."

"Probably proves your point since you forgot they exist."

"That's kinda true."

"You can always be a janitor."

She laughs, bright and eager. "I don't think I can sell that to my parents. They'd both have heart attacks and I'd be an orphan. I'll also inherit, so that's not too bad for a future plan."

"It's a big question. What do you want to be when you grow up?"

"I really don't know."

"I don't actually take history."

"What?"

"I kinda made it up so I have something to talk to you about, that day, when I came to thank you. Then I was kinda committed."

"But you kept saying you're getting As."

"I do. Almost always. Just not for history. Which I kinda don't take."

"So all this time I thought I was helping you."

"You were. Just not in history. I might have killed myself, I think. If you weren't here."

"I don't think you would."

"I don't think so either. But we can pretend you saved my life."

He takes a moment. "Should I be bothered by the lying? I think I should be. But I don't feel like I am."

"That's good. I'm also a virgin."

"Eh?"

"Yup. Zero sexual experience. I got groped but that's it. And that was through a t-shirt and my bra. I mean, besides flashing you every night." She looks at her watch. "I'll kinda be eighteen in two hours. So I'm confessing everything now. Do you want to confess anything?"

"You never said your birthday was coming."

"My birthday doesn't matter. There's only one thing I want from you. I don't know when I decided but I did decide it would be you, that it had to be you, because it had to be someone kind and someone for whom it wasn't just sex and someone who loved me and someone whom I... It had to be you. I can wait, but you have two hours left if you want to deflower a seventeen year old. I think men are supposed to find that hot? You see these ads, horny teen virgins in your area or something like that. I know you don't have Internet–"

"I have Internet."

"Is that hot? Horny teen virgins? It actually sounds very creepy. What do you think?"

"Well... er. I don't..."

"Look at you, I open my legs and you can barely speak. It took me forever before I realised, but I see through you now. I see right through you. You have no idea how to handle this, us. I kinda assumed you knew what you were doing because you're an adult. But you're kinda clueless. I kinda assumed you were right we're not supposed to have sex because it's wrong. But it's not. I don't know how else to convince you and *really*, from what I understand, a girl shouldn't have to try this hard. I even thought of telling you if you don't have sex with me, I'll give my virginity to the first guy who wants it. But one thing I've learnt from all this history is something always gives. And I don't want it to be me but even I know I can't wait for you forever. I can wait. I tell myself I can wait, but it's been months and... yeah. Something always gives.

And remember I said you have to choose between breaking my heart or sleeping with me?"

It takes a moment before he registers the question. "I remember."

"I should have said: 'You have to break my heart or my hymen.'"

"It kinda has a ring to it."

"I know right?"

"Yeah..."

...

...

"Don't you have anything to say?"

"I–"

"Yes?"

He takes a deep breath. "I do love you."

"I love you too." She says it matter-of-factly, as if satisfied facts have been agreed upon.

"But–"

"Oh come on! No buts! I lied about one more thing. I can't wait anymore. I really can't. What you said, about being nice? Anyone can be nice. But you're something else, you're kind. Niceness and kindness, it looks the same, the actions are the same, but to be nice is only an action, and to be kind is... it's kinda something else. It's... character. I don't think anyone has even been so kind to me. Not like you. Not all the time. Not when being kind to me means you have to deny yourself something. It's something else. You're something else. And you have to stop being nice now."

She gets up and goes to the door and locks it. She stands in front of the door. "See me." She unbuttons her blouse and drops it to the floor.

Her skirt follows.

She pulls open a drawer, takes out a note. "I was forced to write this. Those aren't my words."

She tears the note in half, hands it over.

He holds it, unable to take his eyes off her. She unhooks her bra and drops it. "Socks?"

"..."

"On or off. Simple question."

"I... On."

"Read the note."

"Oh." He looks at it: "I will do whatever you want."

He looks up.

"These words are mine now." She pulls the slip of paper from his fingers. "Wet."

She sticks the note on the wall and she climbs on the bed and she gets on her knees in front of him, holding his gaze with sparkling eyes. "You love me."

He nods. He smiles as he realises that is perhaps the truest thing either of them has said. "I do love you."

"I've been waiting for you to figure it out. I've always known."

"Have you?"

"Your room is spotless but you keep those notes on your wall. They're not stuck with icing."

"It's certainly not icing."

"Nobody leaves bodily fluids around like that, it's totally gross."

"It kinda is."

"It's also very sweet. And I love you too."

"I've always known." He really didn't.

"Not very subtle, am I?"

"Were you really going to... you know, give your virginity to the first guy who wants it?"

"No. I just thought of telling you that."

"You can't go around saying just anything to get what you want."

"Yeah, I kinda can though. I'd do anything for you, saying anything is easy. The thing is, the reason I'd do anything for you is you don't want me to do anything at all. I want you to have me because you don't want me. I mean... that sounds as if I want something only because I can't have it, and that's not what I mean. It's like–"

"I know what you mean."

"Do you see me now?"

"Maybe for the first time."

"Have you decided? Break my heart or break my hymen."

"You were waiting to say that."

"I kinda was."

"Yes."

"Is that a yes, you've decided? Or a yes to sleeping with–"

He kisses her.

And then she is...

And then she is *here*.

"Ask me again. Ask me what I want to be when I grow up."

"What do you want to be when you grow up?"

"I want to be with you."

The Weaver's Daughter

"China," he says. "The motherland."

She laughs, looks up from the shirt she is folding. "The motherland, huh? Do you even know which village your family comes from?"

"Of course not. Nobody does. I'm not even sure how many generations ago my forefathers came. But it's still the motherland."

"Okay, dear." She places the folded shirt neatly into the suitcase.

"Did you know any ethnic Chinese can become a Chinese citizen?"

"Why would you want to?"

"Just saying." He stands near her, surveying her work with the nodding approval of one who does not have to do the work. "Why are you bringing bird food?"

"In case I get hungry. It's for Pica, obviously."

"You're bringing your bird on our holiday?"

"Uh-huh. Are you bringing your phone?"

"I can't just take off with no way for the office to contact me. *Why* are you bringing the bird?"

"Pica is important."

"Aren't there laws about this kind of thing? Quarantine and such?"

"There are. It's not a big deal."

"So you've done this before, then?"

"Not exactly. I've gone with Daddy and Pica a few times, when I was much younger. It's fine."

"Your father has brought the bird on holiday *a few times*?"

"Uh-huh." She turns to look at him, her head tilted to the side in thought. "You know, I've brought Pica before, but I've never brought a boyfriend... so you might try to be less noisy than the bird."

He says: "Well, that was strange."

"What was?"

"The girl at the counter, when we checked in. She didn't say anything about the bird."

"You'll see in the morning."

"Hmm. And she didn't count the cash."

"Huh?"

"You paid her in cash, in an envelope. She didn't open it to count it. She just kept it."

"Oh, that. It's... Well. I guess you can say she's family."

"You never mentioned this place is run by your relatives."

"It's... not *exactly* my relatives. I'm really tired, dear. I'll explain in the morning."

"Alrighty. You go to bed, I've to check my email and clear up some work."

"I'm going to shower first. Join me?"

"Let me just check my mail first."

"Fine, whatever."

"This is the life." He leans back against the edge of the pool.

She splashes water at him. The water is warm, though the air is cold. He wipes his face with a hand, is too at peace to retaliate.

"A hot spring in the mountains." He closes his eyes, smiles. "It's just... strangely perfect."

She walks to the edge, leans back next to him. Under the water, her hand finds his.

He points into the distance, where there is a giant cage, housing birds; a riot of feathery colour, even from this distance. "Look, more birds."

"They're magpies. Like Pica."

"I always thought magpies were black and white."

"Some are, not all. You can go look at them."

"Maybe later. But we have time now, tell me the story."

"What story?"

"Why you brought your bird here. Does this place belong to your relatives?"

"One condition."

"Yeah?"

"You don't check your mail for the rest of the day."

"'Till lunch."

"I'll consider that a victory. Well, once upon a time, there was a cowherd..."

The cowherd, as these stories go, lost a calf.

He went in search of it, because (as these stories go), the lost calf is more important than the rest of the herd, which he had to leave behind to search for the one.

So he walked into the woods. After a time, beneath the trees, he heard singing.

The song was as beautiful as it was out of place. It was strange and lilting and melodic and all the other words to describe songs which are heard deep in the forests. The cowherd was torn between the calf (that most important calf of all) and the song. What was he to do? Continue looking for the calf? Or investigate this pleasant aberration?

Unless – *unless* – the clever cowherd thought, the calf had followed the singing (for it had such beauty!), then the one choice would be as both choices.

So the cowherd followed the singing, moving through the woods until the trees part and there, before him, was a hot spring, and, within it, the most beautiful girl he had ever seen.

She was also the first girl he had ever seen naked.

His mouth dropped open and he marvelled.

I would tell you his thoughts; if he had any. For anyone who is male and has been young would know this: There are times when one has no thoughts at all. These times usually involve a woman in a state of undress.

"Now you're just being condescending," he says into her smug smile.

"You know it's true."

"Maybe. Is this even the right story? We're in a hot spring... is this leading up to you saying you're a beautiful woman? Are you going to sing?"

"No," she laughs. "I'm not singing."

"Good, because I'm not a cowherd, though I've always wondered... Why do we Chinese have cowherds when a lot of us are lactose-intolerant? We don't even make cheese."

"To eat them, of course."

"It doesn't seem very practical. We're a practical people."

"Do you want to hear the story or shall we discuss ancient agriculture?"

"Continue."

Our cowherd recovered his senses. He was young and he was male but he was also polite, and a proper upbringing caused him to avert his eyes. He did so quickly, perhaps to somewhat assuage the guilt for having been staring for so long. This quick movement caused two things. First, in his haste, he turned his entire body, causing the leaves to rustle. Second, he saw the robe upon the earth, soft of colour and vibrant like a rainbow, a technicolour dreamcoat.

The first event, the sound, caused the girl in the spring to call out: "Is anyone there?"

The second event caused him to do something uncharacteristic, drastic, even; he picked up the robe, folded it quickly, and hid it within his clothes. Then he called out: "Hello."

"Who's there?"

"I'm just a cowherd, looking for a lost calf."

She left the water, covering herself as best she could with her arms, and walked towards him. The first thing she noticed, of course, was that her robe was missing. "My robe is missing," she said.

The cowherd, gaze still averted, said: "Perhaps my lost calf took it."

"What would a calf do with a robe?"

He shrugged. "Who understands cows?"

She paused a moment, a little confused, then tried an answer: "Maybe a cowherd?"

She sinks into the water, comes up again. "Anyway, I can't remember how it happened, but they fell in love. She's obviously pretty, but I can't remember what she saw in him."

"Maybe she found it flattering someone likes a girl as condescending as herself."

"Dear, if you want to make fun of me, you should at least make sense. The story gave no indication she was in any way condescending." She shakes her head sadly. "At least *try*."

"Maybe he was as handsome as she was pretty."

"I think it's more likely it's one of those 'you've seen me naked, you'll have to marry me' kinda thing. It's an old story."

"Could be. That's why I have to marry you, after all."

"It's unfortunate. Not just for you. Mostly for me. Almost entirely for me."

"If only you hadn't seduced me."

"If only I had known you were already married to your job."

"So they fall in love."

They fall in love, they got married, lived happily, had two beautiful children.

She was, however, a goddess, a daughter of the Jade Emperor, tasked with weaving clouds of many colours. And, as these stories go, unions as these rarely ended well.

One day, while cleaning out their home, she found a box. Within it was her robe. It was a magic robe, made of the stuff from which she weaved coloured clouds – gossamer and silver lining, gold spun from sunlight and the red threads which connect lovers, cotton candy, that kind of thing. It was the magic of the robe which allowed her to come to earth to bathe in the spring those many years ago.

Running her hands over the divine fabric, she realised she missed her parents and decided to return to Heaven for a quick visit.

Time passes differently in Heaven, so the gods had not yet noticed she was gone. But she broke into tears when she sighted her mother, and they had a happy reunion, and all were amazed she had fallen in love, and had wed, and had two beautiful children.

She knew she could not stay for long, because time passes differently in Heaven, but when she wanted to leave her father disallowed it. She had a task to do, he reminded her. With her gone, there would no longer be clouds of many colours.

"I know this story," he says. "It's the cowherd and the weavergirl."

"Then you know how it ends?"

"To stop her from leaving, the Empress of Heaven, her mother, drew out a hairpin and scratched a river across the sky, separating Heaven and Earth. The river is the Milky Way. And, once a year, the lovers reunite on a bridge across the river."

"That's it then."

"But what does this have to do with your bird? Or with anything, for that matter."

"For that, you'll have to wait."

"So your story is this old story everyone knows?"

"Yeah, pretty much."

He shakes his head. "That's... really unsatisfying. It feels like you're playing a trick on me."

"There's no trick. It's hard to explain, but you'll see. I promise."

"You know, I don't really care any more," he waves grandly. "This hot spring, this view, the mountains, being with you. This is a little bit of Heaven. I'll even keep my end of the bargain and I won't check my mail, even though you cheated me."

"I didn't cheat you."

He chuckles, says to the air: "An old love story is your little secret."

"It's not a love story."

"No?"

"People think it is, and I suppose that means that it is. But the moral of the story is..." She gives a small, rueful sound. "I didn't notice this before, but the moral of the story, and thus the great irony of my life, is this: Work is more important than love."

He thinks for a moment, then nods. "Because the weavergirl has to weave, and the cowherd has to herd, for the entire year but for the one day of their reunion."

"Yes."

"Maybe it *is* a love story. They didn't choose to weave or to herd, that choice was made for them. But they did choose each other."

"It's a tragic love story, then."

"I suppose so."

She carries Pica in its cage as they walk up the mountain. It is almost night, and the air is chilly, their breath coming out in little clouds when they speak.

"Isn't the mountain closed at night?" he says.

"It is. But not tonight, not to us."

"There are other people, with birds."

"Yes."

They walk up the mountain, their route taking them off the road, along a concrete path, guided by little lamps placed upon the ground, then off that path, through the woods. Ahead and behind them, they spot other people, small groups or couples, each with a cage and its bird.

The forest opens into a large clearing, a small lake in its centre, part of a stream running through. People are standing around, clustered in small groups, talking amongst themselves. There's an air of anticipation, of expectancy. Some have small children. It reminds him, almost, of being at a concert, at the time before the music starts.

"This is it," she says.

"What are we doing?"

"Waiting."

"Okay, this is starting to feel like a cult of some sort."

"Yes, we're going to sacrifice the birds."

"*What?* Seriously?"

"And then we'll sacrifice our..." She turns to him, slowly breaking into a big grin, "...*guests.*"

"You're kidding, right?"

"Yes." He couldn't see, but he knows she has just rolled her eyes.

"For a moment there, I was worried."

She giggles, then points upwards at the huge expense of night, the Milky Way a line of dark cutting across the field of stars, a river across the sky.

"It's beautiful," he says.

They stand in silence as the minutes pass, looking up at the sky.

"It's a half-moon," he says.

"Uh-huh, it's always a half-moon."

And they stand in silence as the minutes pass, looking up at the sky.

"Here," she says, "hold Pica."

He takes the proffered cage from her, watches curiously as she opens the door. From the corner of his eyes, he sees movement, and he turns to see the other groups holding up their cages, opening the doors.

There must be hundreds of people here, possibly thousands.

Pica hops to the opening, sticks its head out. The magpie turns to face the sky, as if it too understands the precious rarity of this sight, this river of pinpoint lights.

He watches as Pica hops out, takes flight. It joins the other birds who have just left their cages, joins yet more birds flying in from across the sky, their tiny coloured forms like blinking lights, lit by the bright half-moon hanging in the sky.

He watches as the many streams of birds join together, forming one single river, starting from the pool in the centre of the clearing, reaching out across the sky. A thousand, ten thousand, a million birds, forming a river like shimmering cloth.

The thought pokes at him; magpies are not capable of stationary flight, only hummingbirds are. But the thought feels... strangely unimportant. It feels like he is watching a movie and logic didn't quite apply. Not in this clearing, in these woods, on this mountain, under this sky.

He feels her hand find his, their fingers intertwining automatically. A single figure steps forwards from the spectating crowd, steps into the water, slowly walks, then wades, to the ribbon of birds.

His eyes follow the ribbon upwards, the shimmering bodies of coloured birds, like a moving rainbow, all the way up across the sky. From where he stands, it looks like a giant cross; one arm the shimmering birds, one arm the black on twinkling lights of the Milky Way. Standing here, the Milky Way doesn't look that far away.

His eyes glance down and he sees the figure, a man, reach the ribbon of birds. And then he is... walking on them.

He feels conscious of her hand squeezing his, as the man walks upwards – no, along – as the man walks along the river of birds – the bridge of birds – step by step, moving forwards.

Moving upwards, walking up into the sky.

Then he realises what he is seeing – what her story *is* – what he is being allowed to witness. He speaks in a whisper: "Once a year, the lovers reunite on a bridge across the river."

"Yes," she says, her voice soft, soft as down and feather, soft as a coat made of clouds. "The magpies form a bridge across the river, and the cowherd and the weavergirl meet upon the bridge. Once every year."

"Why are you–? How is it you're...?"

"They had two children. Thousands of years ago, they had two beautiful children."

"You're... a descendant?"

"Yes."

His realises his free hand is in his pocket, holding his phone. He hasn't checked his mail for some time, had reached for his phone subconsciously, had been holding it for a while now. And he realises: Perhaps, *this* is why the cowherd forgot all about the missing calf when he saw the girl.

It *is* a love story. Just because the cowherd and the weavergirl didn't have a choice doesn't mean nobody had a choice. The cowherd had to herd, and the weavergirl had to weave, but he was neither of them. He releases the phone.

He has a choice.

He turns to her. She is looking at him.

She is beautiful, like a goddess, bathing in a pool.

No... Perhaps, after all, he doesn't. He had no choice at all. The choice had been made for him.

It is true, there are times when men, young or thousands of years old, have no thought but one; to walk across the bridge of birds, to be with the one you love.

With his free hand, he takes her other hand. "Our children will get to see this," he says to her, building his own bridge by adding a promise.

She smiles. She nods. She looks as happy as he feels.

"Yes. And their children too."

Feetnote:

It's always a half-moon (technically, a night before, and, thus, a sliver off, a half-moon).

http://en.wikipedia.org/wiki/Qixi_Festival

In Japan, the festival is called Tanabata. The cowherd and the weavergirl are called Hikoboshi and Orihime.

Also, about the Sewing Girl – The weavergirl's reward for being good at her job is separation from her lover. The Rumpelstiltskin girl has to weave straw into gold or die. Red Riding Hood, the girl of needles and pins, was eaten by the wolf. And Sleeping Beauty is prophesied to prick her finger on the spindle and (wait for it) die. It's just not very *encouraging*, is it?

Epilogue:

"Hey," he says, "one sews, and the other looks after sows."

"Looks after sows?"

"Female pigs, s-o-w."

"That's pronounced 'sow', rhymes with 'cow'."

"Yeah, I was thinking of the verb, 'reap what you sow'. Okay, I have it. *So*, one sews clothes, and one sows seeds."

"Your jokes aren't as funny when I have to help you think them through."

"'Cow' rhymes with 'sow'; what rhymes with 'hitch'?"

She smiles. "Fuck off."

"I have another one. You're a descendant, a condescending descendant... A condescendant."

She laughs, perfectly.

Witch-Girl: A Wager of Starlight

"All things can be interrupted," she says, "it is the nature of things."

Upon the grass of the field near the airport – deserted, this time of night – Ramiel lies upon his back, looking up at the stars. Upon his outstretched wing, Stacey lies next to him, her body against his; not warm, not cool, but there. She points up at the sky and she says –

"It takes thousands of years for the light from a star to travel across the cold of space to come here, where it dies on the inside of your eyes."

"Don't blink."

"Why?"

"If you blink, then the light from the star falls upon your eyelids and it is gone. Like having feelings for someone who doesn't have feelings for you. A sight, unseen."

"That's beautiful." She climbs up over him, looks into his eyes. "Don't blink."

"This is a moment," he says, without knowing she already knows, without knowing the moment is going into her heart, where it will remain like the light of a distant star: Not big, not bright, but there.

"This is *the* moment," she smiles, "when I win our first staring contest."

"It is *on*, witch."

"Bitch."

"What?"

"'It is *on*, bitch.' That's how you say it."

"I am not going to call you 'bitch'."

"Are you sure?" Her smile spreads slowly. "Don't you want to make me your bitch?"

"I'm not quite sure what that means; I've heard the phrase, but..."

"I don't know either. But I think it involves me being on my hands and knees and–"

"No. I'm sure it involves you making me a sandwich."

"Does that mean I get to use the kitchen?"

"What did we discuss about the kitchen?"

"It is *your* kitchen." She pouts.

"And it follows...?"

"But– Then how am I going to...?"

"Ergo, no bitching."

"Oh fine! What's the wager?"

"What wager?"

"The staring contest. What's the wager?"

"It wouldn't be fair. You can't win a staring contest against a demon."

"Watch me." She beams. "Geddit? Cause it's a staring contest?"

"Yes, Stace. Quis custodiet ipsos custodes?"

"Same to you."

"It means 'Who watches the watchmen?'"

"Oh, *that*. They watch each other. Ready?"

"Quite."

She closes her eyes, her lips slowly widening into a smile. Her eyes open. "Go."

Upon the grass of the field, Ramiel lies upon his back. Stacey is on her hands and knees, over and looking down upon him. She stares.

He smiles. "Don't blink."

Then his vision discolours as his eyes ignite.

She squeals as her hand covers her eyes. "Fuck!" She tumbles onto him.

From the uncomfortably squirming weight upon him, her voice lilts: "I hate you."

And her body ripples, a quivering mess of joy, sending out peals of laughter to echo through the field of stars. She laughs as he pushes her off him, laughs as she lies down beside him, and she laughs as she puts herself in that space between his shoulder and his arm, as she puts her into the space where she belongs.

And it is uncomfortable but that is okay, because the night is beautiful.

And the night is beautiful because the girl is–

–interrupting his internal narrative. Tapping him, impatiently, with her hand.

"Yes?" he says.

"Aren't you going to take your prize?"

"I still win?"

"Of course you do. Triumph by cunning!"

"What's my prize?"

"The usual prize for a hero is he gets the girl."

"I get the girl?"

"You get the girl."

"What does the girl get?"

"Fucked senseless."

"..."

"...?"

"Right now?"

"Yes, idiot! You got the girl. What else do you imagine you might do with her?"

"Tandem cycling."

"Maybe you don't get me after all."

He waits, trying to time it. She'll sulk, and then the thoughts in her head will click into place, and she'll forget she is supposed to be sulking.

"You can't cycle. Why would you even *want* to?"

And the night is beautiful–

"I can make sandwiches, you know. I don't want you to think I can't. Because I *can*. You don't let me. That's *different*."

And the night is beautiful because–

"Fuck it. I don't have to take this lying down. You are getting your fucking prize." She climbs up over him, slips the straps of her dress off her shoulders, looks into his eyes. "There are two puns in what I just said. It was very clever."

"I noticed. Also, while I haven't tried cycling, I think I might be able to do it. One would imagine my wings would cause drag, which might unbalance me, but if you think about it–"

"I don't want to think about you cycling right now."

"Listen, if I spread my wings–"

"If you want to talk, talk to my eyes. Stop telling my boobs about cycling."

He looks up into her eyes. They are rather annoyed. "Alright. So, if I spread my wings–"

"Shut the fuck up."

She leans forwards and upwards, moving her breast to his mouth.

He turns his head slightly to the side. "Are we allowed to say that? Because, let me tell you, the number of times I've–"

She leans back.

He turns back to face her.

"You're doing this on purpose."

"Doing what?"

"You're... You're a sick, depraved bastard."

"Am I?"

"You're frustrating me on purpose."

"Let me tell you about the wings..."

"What wings?"

"When I cycle–"

"Not this again! Are you punishing me for something?"

Blink. "What did you *do*?"

There is, just barely, a pause. "What do you think I did?" she says, not without sounding suspicious.

"Tell me what you did."

"I... Nothing!"

He looks at her. She has her innocent look on.

A moment passes. "I'm not punishing you."

Another moment passes. "You get some kind of sick pleasure out of torturing your girlfriend. I'm a princess, you know, you shouldn't treat me like this."

He runs his hand up her side, over her hip, runs his thumb up the incline of her breast, then, without touching it, in a circle around her areola.

She takes a deep breath. "If... If I let you finish telling me about your stupid bicycle, can we fuck?"

"Okay. If I spread my wings, and cycle, it'd be like a hang glider."

She looks at him. He runs his thumb in that small circle, its orbit unwavering.

"And...?"

"And what?"

"That's it?"

"That's it."

"If you're done teasing me, please touch me?"

Gently, he pinches her nipple.

"♥♥♥"

He pulls her forwards.

She is a squirming mess on top of him. He can feel her smiling, her lips just above his.

She licks his lips. "I hate you."

Upon the grass of the field, she is a squirming mess on top of him.

And it is uncomfortable but that is okay, because the night is beautiful.

And the night is beautiful because the girl is beautiful.

Because she makes all the stars seem a little bit brighter.

The Fish Cannot See The Water

"Time and tide," she says.

His Dome is much like every other; photochromatic glass held by hexagonal frames, like a honeycomb, topped with the metal nipple which receives the microwave stream from the Dyson sphere far above. With a diameter of two hundred metres, even its size is unexceptional.

What is exceptional, however, is the girl.

Her beauty, he knows, is exceptional. And her skill – at what she is doing now – is exceptional, although he will be the first to admit he has limited experience in this regard. He moans, he shudders, that feeling of great and grand relief floods through his body as he releases into her mouth.

"Enough," he says, after a few moments more.

She lifts her head up, looks at him with playful, sparkling eyes – always like moonrise on ocean – and she opens her mouth. Her tongue sneaks out, tendrils of sticky whiteness; her tongue returns, her lips close in, she swallows. She smiles.

"I love you so much right now," he grins.

She laughs, she shakes her head, she rolls her eyes. "And, somehow, I don't find that surprising."

He retracts his legs onto the platform – causing small waves to undulate across the water – takes her hand, shifts himself along the steps. Reaching the spot, he grips the handle with his free hand, carefully pulls her onto the small platform. He leans back, with his legs stretched out and submerged. She rests herself, her lower half beneath the slow spill of the waterfall, her head in his lap, looking up at him, looking down at her.

He pulls her hair away from her face, slicks it behind her ear. Idly, he runs a finger down the side of her face, along the line from cheekbone to jaw, then over the breather over her neck, and he brings his hand to rest upon her breast.

"For someone who says I shouldn't have them," she says, "you really enjoy them too much."

"You evolved, dearest. Deal with it."

She sticks out her tongue.

His voice is tender as he says: "There are no mermaids in the Bible." After the hundredth time you have had the same conversation, it is no longer about the topic, it is about the ritual.

She puts her hand over his, squeezes. "If they don't produce milk. Why would they evolve?"

"Mine don't produce milk."

"The female of your species does."

"My current thesis is they are there to seduce men."

"Your personal experience and, might I add, entertainment, aside, that makes no sense."

"It makes perfect sense."

"The logic might hold for human females, but *we* don't produce milk. Our breasts have no bearing on fertility."

"That you know of."

"You're a really bad scientist."

He leans in, and he kisses her upon the forehead. "Coming from a Creationist, I'm not sure if that's a compliment or an insult."

"It's an insult, dearest. You can't have a thesis and find evidence for it. You need at least some evidence before you formulate your thesis."

"That's what I said about Professor Jed."

"I know. It is. I learn fast. Why do you think it is you love me?"

"Oh, I don't know," he grins, he squeezes, "an idea comes to mind. An idea comes to hand, rather."

She giggles, even as she shakes her head. "Am I important to you?"

"The most important thing of all."

"And you to me. But we can't have children. Ergo, if evolution made sense, we shouldn't be in love."

"That's the same logic they use to claim homosexuality isn't natural, because homosexuals can't breed. It's been disproved."

"No. Our love depends on it."

"I know you feel so."

"God wants me to be happy, and so He wants me to love you, and to be loved by you."

He kisses her again. "I thank your God."

She closes her eyes, she smiles; the quiet, peaceful smile of the joy of the calm sea. "The thing about you, which I adore... is that... while you think my faith is stupid, you make me believe you believe."

"I believe in you."

They float in the centre of the pool, looking up at the night sky, through the grid of the Dome, anchored each to the other by fingers intertwined.

"When I was young," he says. "My sisters used to go prawning. It's like fishing, with prawns. It's this little concrete pool, not like this one, above the ground, like a fountain."

She listens.

"I only went the one time. You fish with rods, with worms as bait. You fish the little buggers out, and you pull off their pincers, and you put them back in a net in the water, to keep them alive, keep them fresh. You pay for time, an hour or two, and when you're done, you take your net out of the water, and you skewer each poor sod on a little wooden stick. Then you pop him, still alive, onto the barbecue.

"I went a few times, my sisters liked it. I found it horrific, intellectually, not that it made me physically sick or anything, I just found it intellectually repulsive. Borderline creepy, I suppose. I explained it to my sisters, but they didn't get it. It's because they're crustacea. Prawns, shrimp. They're not like us.

"From the viewpoint of the prawn, he was lucky enough to find something to eat, and then he got dunked into water, he started drowning, his arms were pulled off. He returns to the air, miraculously, and he thinks he has freedom, but he's trapped in a net, or maybe he's in so much pain from having his limbs yanked out he doesn't even realise he's trapped in a net.

"Then he's drowning again. And impaled, a wooden shaft pushed through him. Lengthwise, not just stabbed, but impaled. Then comes the fire."

There is a moment of quiet.

"We won't ever do that to kittens. But we do it to prawns because we can't hear them scream, because they're not mammals, like us. Crustacea."

I'm not a mammal, she thinks, and this story... it says a lot about people, humans and mermen, mammals or not. But, mostly, it says a lot about you.

"I love you," she whispers.

"What you said earlier," he begins, "about boobs?"

"That you should be less fixated?"

"It's like long hair. It's a marker of femininity."

She takes a moment. "Not bad, scientist."

"There you go."

"Now all you need to do is prove it."

"The bathysphere project," he says, "that I was telling you about? It just got funding. I already applied for a transfer."

"Oh no!" she replies with mock horror. "What about your life's mission to destroy all which I believe in?"

"Are you seriously making fun of me for doing this for you?"

"Aww! Don't get mad. I'm sorry. It's really sweet."

"Damn right it is. I submit to you; how is God fair, if you can come here, but I can't go to New Atlantis?"

"You can," she says coyly, "if you join a mission. God wants you to."

"I really don't get that. How is the only humans who can afford to live there permanently belong to the Church?"

"As you've repeatedly told me, we're a naive lot."

"I simply do not understand how the government can think this to be unimportant. There are so many advances just waiting to be made; scientifically, of course, culturally –"

"Of course, dearest," she says soothingly.

"It's not that I don't like the work here. But I didn't become a scientist to compile data all day, you know?"

"I thought you became a scientist to meet young, naive, mermaids who swallow."

He smiles. She does that to him. She makes him smile. "You do swallow."

"I don't get why humans don't."

"You can't taste salt."

"That's true."

A moment passes.

"Hey!" she says. "Does that mean you peed in my pool again?"

"No," he laughs. "It was just the one time."

"But you didn't tell me for weeks! Do you know how disgusting that is?!"

He nods. "I do, actually. You keep telling me."

She settles.

A moment passes.

And she says: "I am a naive mermaid, aren't I? Poor me, taken in by an evil human who only uses me for my body."

But still she smiles.

"Don't worry too much about this," she says. "You'll hate New Atlantis."

"I'll love it there."

"No, you only think you will. Once you actually have to live there... it'll be different. You'll be cooped up in small little spaces. There's no sky, not like here."

He looks up through the glass of the Dome. "I don't see what the big deal is."

"Light. It's all dark, down there. The videos you've seen, it's not like that at all. It's all romanticised. You think it'll be like here, but... it won't. It's not like moving from one city to another."

"And here's where you say your eyes are proof of Creation."

"I wasn't going to, and they are, but... I'm serious. You'll hate it there."

"But you miss it."

"I *don't* miss it. I miss my family, that's all. Steam-based technology, if you can even call it 'technology'. I think… it looks interesting to you, but… no metal, no electricity, and the food. You'll hate the food. And the racism is really bad, they still don't allow interspecies marriage."

"That's because of the Church."

"I know… but…"

"And it's not like I don't get called 'fishfucker' every day."

"It's worse, down there. It really is. They kill people like us. More often than they do here."

"Why are you doing this?"

"I don't want you to get your hopes up, that's all."

"Don't you want to go home?"

"I am home."

"Okay," he says. But he didn't really mean it. She could always tell.

Sometimes she feels he's the one who isn't home.

"I thought about what you said," she says, "about the Church being the only permanent group of humans in New Atlantis."

"And…?"

"It's because there's nothing down there."

"Hmm."

"There would be tourism, wouldn't there? But it's too expensive, it's too dangerous, and there's simply nothing to see."

"Hmm."

He's still not convinced. She could tell.

They float in the middle of the pool, at night.

"Hey," she says.

He turns to her. She's pointing at the dark circle of metal at the apex of the Dome, the base of the nipple.

She moves her hand across the air, waving across an imaginary arc. "I always find it amazing, when I think about it."

"The Dyson sphere?"

"Yeah. Collecting sunlight from space, beaming it down. Thousands of streams, all invisible, each one of them a bridge across the sky."

He listens.

"A sphere around the earth," she says. "Like the surface is a sphere around the ocean. But there are no invisible bridges."

"You're an invisible bridge."

"Connecting you to New Atlantis?"

"Yes."

"If you believe in God, then we're all invisible bridges."

He squeezes his fingers, around hers. "We used to believe God was a figure in the sky. Then we conquered the skies and there was no God there."

"He's there."

"So now we believe God is somewhere beyond the universe, outside looking in."

"He is."

"And He sees clouds of nebulae and solar storms and spiral galaxies, and, somewhere, smaller than an atom compared with the Earth, is this planet, this little blue sphere, this third rock from Sol, and, smaller than an atom compared with the Earth, is this little dome. And inside it is you."

"He sees you too."

"Somewhere, beyond the sky where we didn't find God, are clouds of nebulae and spiral galaxies, and us, this tiny little things, so small compared with the great vastness we might as well not exist, we took photos. Of nebulae clouds and the surface of our nuclear sun and lines and lines of stars, curling through the dark. And we find these things beautiful. Why would we find them beautiful, I think, why should we? It is a sight the apes, coming down from the trees, were never meant to see. Why would we see this, and think it possessing of a great and subtle beauty?"

The water ripples as she turns towards him. "Are you saying what I think you're saying?"

"No. Of course not. Lying here, looking up, I can't help but think it. But then I look at you and I know exactly why I find you beautiful, and I know evolution is true."

"Idiot."

She smiles. You believe, dearest, I believe you do. It's not God you cannot stand. It's the Church.

She pushes herself away from him and swims out of his reach.

"I'm not going back," she declares.

"Why?! After all the hoops I've jumped through –"

"Open your eyes! You grew up on this romantic notion of mermen; those stories are just fairy tales! Written by humans who haven't even met us, much less seen New Atlantis! Why do you think there are so many of us here?! Why do you think fully a third of mermen are in the sex trade? We want to get away!"

He is stunned into silence. It is very clear to her he had not expected her anger. He had come bearing what he was certain was good news.

"Listen," she says, slowly, trying to calm herself. "Just listen. I studied English for years, do you know why? Because my mother made me. Because taking this five year bond with the Institute is the only way to the surface for a girl which wouldn't end up in a brothel. There are millions of us down there, all miserable in the dark. We don't even have the technology to surface on our own! Do you get that? New Atlantis is nothing like what you think it would be. Nothing! It's– It's– like a village in Tibet or Africa or something – you can understand that, right? – all you've seen are pictures with colourful costumes. Living there is totally different! And New Atlantis is far worse than any place on the surface can ever be."

She looks at him, her head above the water, just beyond his reach.

"Those stories aren't real," she says plaintively.

His tone, like his face, is devoid of emotion as he says: "They only want me because of you. Your bond ends in a year. This is a two year expedition, and they only agreed to take me because I assured them you would come with me, and extend your bond for another year."

"I'm not going back."

"You have to," he insists.

"God, I can't believe I ever thought it was cute, your fascination with us. You're obsessed! I let you prattle on with your delusions because I didn't have the heart to tell you the truth. It's not even an obsession, it's a damn fetish with you!"

And she regrets the words even as she says them: "You really are a fishfucker!"

He looks so hurt her heart breaks.

She swallows, whispers: "The last thing which my mother said to me was this: 'Don't ever look back.' She wants me to meet someone nice and get married and spawn, here, on the surface. She talks about the freshwater pool, *this* freshwater pool. She has never been in one, will never know what it feels like. She was as obsessed as you are."

He's holding up something. There is a brief glint of metal. It dangles from his hand, falling-unfolding, a chain, with something on it. His hand opens. It falls into the water.

A moment passes.

She dives down after it.

The force of her passage pushes it away from her, towards the wall of the pool.

Whatever it was, it seems to have disappeared. She looks, first, towards one of the small metal grills which pulls the water out. It's not there.

She's out of oxygen.

She surfaces, feels her gills flaring in her breather as she takes a deep breath.

He's not there.

She looks around, her eyes wide, drowning in panic.

"Don't go!" she calls out, to his back.

In a moment, she turns to the chair, looks back down into the pool; torn between going after him and finding the dropped chain.

She flares her gills again. Instinct has already made her choice. Get it before the filters get it.

She dives down.

Down.

There.

Caught by one of the grills. It sparkles.

She surfaces.

She swims to the edge of the pool.

She looks at the closed door through the diamond ring in her fingers.

"What were you thinking?" she whimpers, her voice broken. "To ask my father for my hand?"

She turns again to the chair. He has forbidden her from using it alone. She knows exactly why. For the same reason she can't have him go to New Atlantis. It's just too dangerous. Why doesn't he see that?

She can't use the chair. She won't disobey. You don't have to be married to be a good wife.

A good wife.

She can feel the ring, clenched in her fist, the diamond biting into her flesh.

"This..." she whispers, sobs. "This is both the sweetest and the most bloody stupid thing I've ever imagined. You stupid, beautiful man... What were you thinking? If I swim through that door with a human boyfriend... Do you imagine you'd be welcomed as I was by your parents? You're so spoilt and sheltered, you are, you. You... Me... It would break my mother's heart. And my father would kill you."

He's not here, of course.

There's no one to listen to her.

She can feel the small movement of something on her face.

Her fist reaches up, wetness upon her cheek. Her fist, and its treasure, moves – awkwardly, uncaringly – smearing the wet across her lips.

There's no one to taste her tears.

She can't taste them herself, of course.

Her tears are salty, human tears; they have no taste on a mermaid's tongue.

The Frog Prince: A Love Story

"**F**rogs aren't supposed to talk," she says.

"I'm not a real frog," says the frog. It puffed itself up. "I used to be a prince."

"Prince of what? Lily pads?"

"Spain, actually."

"Spain has princes? I find that hard to believe."

"It's true, whether or not you believe it."

"Not that Spain has royalty, that you're part of it. But, say I believe you, why are you a frog? Did a witch do this to you?"

"I don't know if she was a witch. The thing is, I wasn't a very nice prince. I came here on holiday, went to a club, took a girl back to my hotel, did our thing, then I asked her to leave. When I woke up the next day, I was this."

"That's horrible! You deserved it, you monster."

"I know." The frog looks down, and she feels a tinge of pity. It looks up again, back at her with its large froggy eyes: "But I've learnt my lesson! Don't I deserve a second chance?"

"I'm not going to kiss you."

"I can smell your perfume. We have a very advanced sense of smell."

"What does my perfume have to do with anything?"

"A girl who wears perfume to school? I'm sure your lips have come into contact with more disgusting things than a frog."

She leans back, eyes never leaving the frog on the table, leans forwards again, placing her face close to it. Her eyes narrow, an eyebrow rises: "Did you just call me a slut?"

"I'm just saying. No judgement."

"That's not a very effective way of convincing someone to help you, you know."

The frog clasps its hands together in pleading supplication. "I'm sorry! Please, will you give me a quick peck on the lips? To save me from this cruel fate? Err... you're very pretty."

"Well. Okay, I guess –"

She recoils as the fist, with a flash of silver, comes down over the frog.

The hand returns to its owner, who is standing next to the table.

She looks back down. The frog is impaled to the table by a scalpel through its head. Its eyes are still open. She turns away.

The frog-slayer leans in close to her, and his voice is barely audible: "Come by tonight, around nine."

"Yes, sir."

He points at the frog. "At least pretend to cut it, though I'm sure you'll get an A."

"I'm sure you'll make me earn it," she winks.

He straightens up, turns to leave, turns back to her. "Oh, were you talking to the frog?"

She shakes her head. "Frogs aren't supposed to talk."

Victoria

 $\mathbf{M}$ y name is Victoria and I stand before the old lady and I don't know who she is, or why she is standing before me.

My name is Victoria and I say to the old lady: "Shall we talk?"

She reminds me of my mother, which reminds me, strangely, of my very first memory.

My name is Victoria and my hair is red and my eyes are green. This is not important, except in a place where nobody has red hair or green eyes, then it becomes the only thing important.

Their hair is dark here, as are their eyes.

As a child, I came home crying one afternoon. One of the boys, the neighbours' children I played with, had called me a word which he had just learnt from his mother. And all the kids had pointed their fingers at me, and said the word, over and over. Pointing and laughing, laughing and pointing. A pointed finger, a pointed word.

My mother, as mothers do, calmed me down, held me tight until I stopped shaking, wiped the tears from my eyes, and, as mothers do, asked me what's wrong.

"What did the word mean?" I asked of her.

She shook her head. "You're not old enough to understand," she told me, in that soothing way of hers. "But never ever say it, and, most especially, never ever let your father hear it leave your lips. Do you understand me, child?"

I nodded.

And she hugged me close, smoothed my hair, and whispered to me: "Do not think overmuch of the other children. They're not like you."

They're not like me, she had said, and it was true.

My name is Victoria and I was born in Ireland in 1838. This is not important, except to the parents to whom this child was born, then it becomes the only thing important.

It was the year after the Queen for whom I was named ascended the throne. They call her Queen Victoria, but, truly, she was an Empress, for there was no doubt Britain was an Empire. And it was in service to Britannia my father, a mere clerk, brought his family, including his one infant daughter, to Singapore.

Why, I had asked my mother – for I only saw my father at dinner, and he rarely addressed my presence – why are we here? Are there no other clerks with families? Why does no one else have hair the colour of mine?

She told me I had been a sickly child, which was true, and my father was afraid for my health, which was only half true.

What was wholly true was he was afraid, not of my health, but of me.

My name is Victoria and I stand before the old lady and I don't know who she is, or why she is standing before me.

My name is Victoria and I say to the old lady: "Shall we talk?"

My name is Victoria and I first fell in love when I was seventeen. This is not important, except to the girl it was happening to, then it becomes the only thing important.

In 1855, we were fighting the Russian War; but that was far and far away. I did not know to care, but the father who never spoke to me looked wan, which worried me, but even those worries evaporated like so much morning mist when I was with him.

Him.

They say you always remember the first man who breaks your heart. It has been over a hundred years, so I can attest this to be true.

How dashing he was, and how clever. At least I assume so, I cannot remember how he was, why I loved him with all my heart. That is not important. That did not matter. What mattered was he was Chinese; what mattered was I was not.

I had gone to dinner to meet his family. I thought it went well.

But the evening after that he said to me: "I cannot see you anymore."

What strange words to tell a girl who saw before her a future filled with rainbows and birds.

Talking, of course. Talking, and crying, and plaintive looks and pleading words.

And his mother had said to him: "That girl shall never marry into this house."

Why? Why? *Why?*

His parents, he had said, had an arranged marriage. That he himself would choose his bride was leeway enough given to these modern times. That bride had to be Chinese.

But... I'm sure there's something we could do to change her mind.

And here he shakes his head. You don't understand, he told me. She didn't say "that girl". The word she had used was certain and scornful. It meant her mind was not to be changed.

He stands up, and he looks at me, and the very last words he says to me are these: "I'm sorry."

They're not like me, my mother had said, and it was true.

What is also true, terribly terribly true, is this –

If they are not like me, then it follows – then it *must* follow – I am not like them.

My name is Victoria and I sleep in the soil. This is not important, except in a world where no one else does, then it becomes the only thing important.

After my heart broke, I went to the hill with the fort. The woods always calmed me. The earth, covered in dead leaves, soft and almost springy to the step, that strange quality to the air; moist, almost cool, and the not-quite quiet of civilisation muffled by trees.

Part way up the hill I found a spot where I could see the sky, and, with my heart broken, I cared not about dirtying my dress, all I wanted was to lie down. And so I did.

Looking up at the sky, the tears flowed from my eyes as I remembered, as I wished, as I hoped, as I do all the things in my head people do when they could no longer do things with their heart.

It was a sort of madness.

In my grief – Ah! But the first breakup of any relationship is never truly possessed completely by grief, because there is always a glimmer of hope, of reconciliation; and more so the first breakup of one's first relationship – nonetheless, hopeful or otherwise, I was grieving, and, in that grief, I sunk into the earth.

I sunk into the earth as one would sink into a pile of pillows; slowly, to be surrounded by softness.

At first, I did not realise this was happening, and, when I did, instead of panic, I felt a calmness, a stillness, and I let it continue, sinking in slowly, until the leaves covered my eyes, and I fell asleep.

In the morning, when I went home to my worried mother, my dress was clean. The dirt and leaves did not stick to my clothes nor my skin. It was as if the earth itself was a blanket, a piece of cloth to be put on or removed.

I thought it was a dream.

My name is Victoria and I stand before the old lady and I don't know who she is, or why she is standing before me.

My name is Victoria and I say to the old lady: "Shall we talk?"

My name is Victoria and I am an elf. This is not important, except in a world of humans, then it becomes the only thing important.

The night I announced to my family I was engaged, my mother came into my room and she told me the single, most defining thing about me.

The elves, she said, would trade a human child for one of their own.

You are, she said, a changeling. An elf, a faerie.

I was a normal baby until I was two. Then I started falling sick, crying incessantly. My worried father came home one night with a cross on a piece of string. He put it around my neck. By morning, my skin under the cross had blistered and burned, red welts clearly in the shape of the cross.

It was a cheap cross, made of iron. Iron is poison to the fae, like lead or mercury or uranium to humans.

I was always sick because in the 1840s, iron was everywhere. Food was cooked in an iron pot. I ate with an iron spoon, washed with an iron basin.

So they replaced what they could with wood, and the child I was stopped falling sick so often, stopped crying.

But that means, I said to my mother, that you're not... and found myself unable to continue.

You're my child, she said to me, with a ferocity which had no room for doubt.

I nodded.

It was true.

It needed to be.

Because what my mother did not say was this – this is why my father stopped speaking to me, could barely stand to look at me.

She is my mother, she had said, and it was true.

It was true.

My name is Victoria and I do not age. This is not important, except I loved someone who did, then it becomes the only thing important.

There is, perhaps, one silver lining to being here, a stranger in the land I grew up in; there were no neighbours to judge me. Cosmetics were frowned upon in London, where my namesake the Queen had gone so far as to publicly declare it improper, vulgar.

And so it was I dressed in greys, and kept my red hair covered, and powered my lips and cheeks to make them lose their vibrancy. I would have wrinkled my skin if I could.

I came to hate my youth, ever afraid the man I loved would come to resent me for it.

But this is... not important.

What is important is this: We had many years together, and there is little to say about happiness because... happiness is when you *just are.*

Nothing.

Nothing need be said, nothing *can* be said. Happiness – prolonged happiness, not the euphoria of first love or winning the lottery or some such event, transient as an orgasm – is the purest state when you are *you*, without pretence, without need or desire, because all you need or desire is there, within your grasp. And you are left with...

Nothing.

Just you.

Floating in the softness.

Without even the words to express the joy, just a sense this would never end, as the days pass too quickly, as the days sped onwards to the anointed time when, yes, without a doubt, the end has to come.

The days pass too quickly as the man I loved grew old while I stayed young. While I looked in the mirror and saw my red hair, never fading to grey, at my skin which never wrinkled, however much I smiled.

I smiled a lot.

Until the time came when I stopped smiling.

My name is Victoria and I stand before the old lady and I don't know who she is, or why she is standing before me.

My name is Victoria and I say to the old lady: "Shall we talk?"

My name is Victoria and the love of my life died in 1888. This is not important, except to the one he left behind, then it becomes the only thing important.

The only thing important. The only thing which mattered at all.

I was sixty, when he died. He was sixty-four. The girl in the mirror looks no more than twenty-five.

How hateful it is to be so young and to bear the joy of a life lived, the burden of a love lost.

We had moved house by then. Twenty years ago, we had moved so the neighbours would not talk, and I became his live-in nurse, for an imagined illness which became a real one.

They are not like me, I am not like them. They can live as a wife to a husband she adores. I have to pretend.

Pretend to be human.

Why do I have to pretend to be human when this pain is oh so human?

This is not a pretend pain. This is not an elfin pain. This is the pain of a human heart.

There is no answer.

But this is true: It was his wife, and not his nurse, who closed his eyes for the last time, barely able to see through the tears of her own.

But this is true: My name is Victoria and this is the man I love.

And so they put him in the ground.

I stood before the tombstone and I asked myself: How? How can it be one man's life is reduced to a single piece of rock, no more than two dates, a beginning and an end.

How can it be our entire life together gets reduced to one line: "Beloved husband."

Yet this is true: My name is Victoria and he is my beloved.

I stood before the tombstone and I felt somewhere in the earth beneath me, so near, is the man I love. Except it is not him. Where is he, then?

Where is he?

There is no answer, is there? If there is a Heaven, how does one who never ages enter Heaven? How does she reunite with the one whom time had stolen from her?

Why is she given youth if it is not also given to him she loved?

Why did God hate me so much He punished me with red hair which never turns to grey? What sin had I committed that I was to be locked away, separated from the humanity I had no choice but to live in?

The humanity I felt but did not live, the humanity which beat in my heart but would not wrinkle my skin.

There is no answer.

This is grief then. A nothing. Not even hope.

I turned around and I walked towards a large tree. It was a few feet away from his grave, and I could still see it, from under its shade.

Then I lay down, and let the earth enfold me.

My name is Victoria and I sleep in the soil.

Like my beloved, I sleep in the soil.

It was true.

My name is Victoria and I stand before the old lady and I don't know who she is, or why she is standing before me.

My name is Victoria and my hair is red and my eyes are green. The old lady has white hair.

You're not like me, I think to her.

It is dark here, because it is night; it is bright here, because there are artificial lights like little moons, scattered all around through buildings so tall they should not be standing. How many years have passed?

Where is the grave I had left behind? There is nothing but grass there, a hill without trees. Where is the tree I had slept under for so long? Why had I not awakened when it was uprooted?

There is a sound like a hum, but loud, like muted thunder, and I look up to see… a train, moving on top of a… a long bridge. They had built tracks in the air.

Is that why?

I look back at the old lady and I ask her: "Is that why? The trains? Are the trains why?"

My name is Victoria and I stand before the old lady.

You're not like me, I think to her, but it is not true.

Why would they build trains here? Where would they go? Where would these trains on this bridge across the sky go?

There is a roar as another train passes, bright and lit as it cuts through the night, how very very fast.

I've never liked trains; they run on tracks of iron.

Is that why?

If you bind the earth in chains of iron, does it sever the link between the earth and those who would sleep in it?

My name is Victoria and I stand before the old lady. I know who she is, but I don't know why she is standing before me.

She is like me. She is exactly like me.

My name is Victoria and my hair is white and my eyes are... I cannot see what colour they are.

in subtle blue, the dawn unfolds

In subtle blue, the dawn unfolds,

  close the windows, one by one;
try and sleep now, unopposed,
  the dreams that run before the sun;

the dreams that run before the sun,
  bounce away now, two by two;
a shepherd's job is never done,
  herding dreams in subtle blue;

herding dreams in subtle blue,
  inside a box now, three by three;
safe from the light now, rule by rule,
  as safe as every dream must be;

as safe as every dream must be,
  keep them in now, four by four;
within the heart-box, under key,
  hidden behind the hidden door;

hidden behind the hidden door;

keep them in now, four by four;

as safe as every dream must be;

inside a box now, three by three;

herding dreams in subtle blue;

bounce away now, two by two;

the dreams that run before the sun;

close the windows, one by one.

Red: The Colour of Her Creation (Pins and Needles)

In a hotel lobby, an elevator dings, its doors sliding open. The girl curls her fingers around the man's elbow, her long red nails digging into the folds of his sleeve as she guides him into the open box.

"Once upon a time," she tells her story, her voice soft and slow, "a little girl was sent upon an errand, to deliver a basket of bread and milk to her grandmother."

The doors of the elevator shut behind them. She presses the button for their floor and he spins her around, pushing her against the mirrored wall. "You're a kinky one. Are we role-playing?"

"The little girl walked into the woods." She smiles, but the man isn't looking at her face: His eyes and his hands are busy, setting free the hooks on her coat.

"In the woods, she met a wolf."

Her coat is a deep red, its hood lined with white fur. The hood is pulled low over her face, the fur contrasting against two strands of auburn hair, framing her shadowed face with white and red.

"'Where are you going, what do you bring?' asked the wolf of the little girl." The last of the hooks release, she pushes him gently back.

"'I bring bread to my grandmother's cottage,' the little girl replied." One palm upon his chest, her other hand pulls down the zipper from her throat. She feels his heart beat through the palm of one hand, feels the slow clicks of the zipper rippling through the fingers of the other.

"'Will you take the Path of Needles or the Path of Pins?' the wolf asked," as her coat spread open beneath the spreading teeth of the zipper, slowly revealing the ascending curves of her breasts. Her smile widens as he draws in a sharp intake of breath, signalling his realisation she is wearing nothing under her red coat.

He is no longer pushing forward, she withdraws the hand from his chest. The fingers on both her hands slide along the opened zipper, moving up and down, lightly dancing upon its metal lines.

The elevator dings, jerks to a stop. Her fingers close around the edges of the coat, she slides the cloth open as the doors part. Her hands follow the rise of her breasts, slowing to a stop as she reveals a hint of the circle at one peak.

Then she reaches down and pulls the zipper up, stopping when it reveals just enough, just barely enough.

"'I'll take the other path and we'll see who gets there first,' said the wolf," as her hand curls around his elbow once again, and he is guided out of the elevator, into the empty corridor.

"Obviously, it was the wolf who reached her grandmother's cottage first. He let himself in, and, in a single great bite, cleaved her grandmother in twain." She can feel his eyes looking down into the shadow and the red of her coat, trying to get a clearer glimpse, a deeper look.

"The wolf ate her grandmother, save for some of her flesh, which he put in a dish, and for some of her blood, which he put in a bottle. Then the wolf dressed himself in her grandmother's shawl, climbed into bed, pulled the blankets up. And waited."

They arrive at the room. Standing before the door, he fumbles in his pockets. She leans into his back, pressing herself against him as he finds the keycard. "The wolf waited," as she whispers into his ear, "for that was all he could do. He waited, impatiently."

He slides the card through the sensor, pulls the door handle down with a firm click.

"The little girl arrived at the cottage, and knocked on the door." She raps her knuckle on the door; once, twice, even as it is already swinging open.

She curls herself around him. "'Come in,' said the wolf," as she pulls him by the lapels of his coat into the room.

"The little girl didn't know the wolf was a wolf.

"'My mother sent me with bread and milk,' said the girl.

"'Put them in the pantry, child. Are you hungry?' asked the wolf," as she pushes him onto the bed, then walks over to an end table, upon which stands a single decanter of wine, deep and dark and red.

"'Yes, Grandmother, I am,' said the girl.

"'Cook the meat in the dish,' said the wolf," as she opens the bottle and pours the wine, darkness spilling into one glass, then another.

"'Are you thirsty?' asked the wolf," as she turns around, holding a glass, leaving its twin upon the table. He had removed his coat and tie, unbuttoned his shirt. Leaning against pillows stacked against the headboard, his eyes follow her across the room.

"'Yes, I am, Grandmother,' said the little girl," as she stops at the edge of the bed, close to him. She holds the glass by its stem, slowly swirling the wine within. Again, a hand pulls the zipper downwards.

This time, only one hand pulls the coat open. This time, she does not stop until one breast was fully revealed to his hungry eyes.

"'Then drink the wine upon the table, child,' said the wolf," as she dips her finger into the wine, swirls it in a circle. She curls her finger within, brings it out, carrying within her long red nail a drop of wine.

"The little girl cooked the meat." She presses the wine onto her nipple, her finger moving in a widening arc, spreading the wine around her areola, the liquid causing her nipple to glisten in the light.

She cradles her breast with her hand. She leans forward, he does the same. "The little girl ate the meat," she whispers, as his mouth closes over her nipple.

A gasp escapes her lips, she runs her fingers through his hair. A moment passes, then she pulls back. She brings the glass into his gaze and he takes it from her. His eyes do not leave her breast, and so he does not notice, upon her forearm, the scars, like tiny Xs, white on white in the shape of a crescent.

"While the little girl was eating, a cat came up to her and said: 'You are eating the flesh of your grandmother!'" She walks back to the table, sits down in one of the chairs next to it.

"'Throw your shoe at the noisy cat,' said the wolf," as she loosens a shoe, dangles it by her toes, tosses it into a corner. She smiles as he does the same. "And the little girl did."

Her gaze holding his, she runs a finger around the rim of the glass of wine upon the table. She picks up the glass, holds it up, as if in a toast, takes a sip. She smiles when he takes a drink. "And while the little girl drank the wine, a bird came up to her and twittered: 'You are drinking the blood of your grandmother!'

"'Throw your other shoe at the noisy bird,' said the wolf," as she removes her other shoe, tossing it, too, into the corner, smiling as he follows. "And the little girl did."

"'Are you cold, child?' asked the wolf.

"'Yes, Grandmother, I am,' replied the girl.

"'Then take off your clothes, come to bed, and I shall warm you up,' said the wolf," as she stands, her toes curling into the carpet, turns to face away from him.

"'Where shall I put my apron, Grandmother?' asked the little girl.

"'Put it on the fire, child, for you won't need it anymore,' replied the wolf," as she bends slightly forwards, to completely unzip her coat.

"'Where shall I put my bodice, Grandmother?' asked the little girl.

"'Put it on the fire, child, for you won't need it anymore.' She repeated the question for each piece of clothing and received the same answer, and she threw each item onto the fire. 'Now, child, come to bed,' said the wolf," as she flaps her coat outward, and turns around.

His eyes travel up the length of her legs, over the nakedness of her sex, over the rise of her breasts, to the smile on her face, and then back down again. Her eyes remain shadowed in her hood, white fur and red hair framing her smile, white teeth and red lips.

She walks back to where she stood, at the edge of the bed, close to him. He leans forward, she places a finger upon his lips, holding him gently back.

She removes her finger from his lips, points it at his free hand, curling it into a hook. He brings his hand up. She picks up his forefinger, guides it to the glass he is holding, dips it into the wine, uses it to coat the wine, once again, around her nipple.

He leans forwards, eyes focused, mouth open. She places his finger across his lips, shaking her head gently when his eyes look up at hers.

She brings his finger down between her legs, moans as it easily enters her. A moment passes, then she pulls it out, brings his finger up to her other nipple, spreads the wetness around it.

He looks up at her, and she gives him a single nod, and his mouth closes over her nipple as his hands cover her breasts.

She speaks through little moans and subtle gasps: "The little girl climbed into the bed, and said to the wolf, 'Grandmother, how hairy you are!'"

She pushes him back against the pillows, walks around the bed to stand near his feet. "'The better to keep you warm, child,' replied the wolf," as she moves his legs apart, crawls onto the bed between them.

"'Grandmother, what big ears you have!' exclaimed the little girl.

"'The better to hear you with, child,' replied the wolf," as she unbuckles his belt, tugs down his pants, tosses them aside.

"'What big...' she encircles his cock with her fingers, licking her lips as she strokes it, "'...eyes you have!'"

"'The better to see you with, child,' replied the wolf," as she bends her head lower, until she is hovering with her mouth a breath away from his cock.

"'And what sharp teeth you have,' said the little girl."

A moment passes.

"Tell my story," she says at last, and her tongue flicks out.

"'The better–'" He gulps, clears his throat "'–to eat you with!'" And she engulfs him in her mouth.

"And he swallowed her whole," he continues, his speech fractured by pleasure: "The wolf ate the little girl. But a passing hunter came by. The hunter killed the wolf. He cuts open the belly of the wolf. He sets her free!"

She stops, lifts her head to look him in the eyes. "A hunter. What a stupid ending." She climbs above him, lowers herself onto him.

Moments pass, as she moves herself, as his hands grab at her, her waists, her breasts..

Then he says: "Why is the ending stupid?"

She leans forward, still moving, until her lips are next to his ear: "Men always think the only possible solution for evil men is good men."

And moments pass, as she moves herself, as she moans into his ear.

And he says: "You never said which path she took, the Path of Needles or the Path of Pins."

"Hush."

And still she moves, until, finally, her release comes, and her body shudders, and she smiles, satisfied.

She pushes herself up on straightened arms, her hands upon the headboard above his shoulders.

He thrusts his hips, lifting her up slightly. "Now that you're finished..."

She moves, slowly. "I've been with many men like you."

"I got that impression. Now come on."

"There are those who don't care if the woman cums and those who do. Those who do like knowing they're good in bed. They don't really care about the woman. They're just pretending."

"Whatever."

"'Will you take the Path of Needles or the Path of Pins?' the wolf asked," as she smiles, a satisfied smile; brilliant and full of teeth. "I don't remember. What does it matter which path I took?"

She leans back, moving her hips in small circles. "What girl could outrun a wolf? It's a false choice, an illusion of free will; both paths were equally prickly."

With both hands, she reaches behind her head, releasing her hair. Her clenched hands each holds a hairpin, its metal length reaching out between her fingers, long and shiny in the light. "Both paths were equally fatal."

He doesn't notice or doesn't care. "Just lie down so I can fuck you."

"Don't be impatient. I'll make sure you're finished."

Then the pins are in his neck; the ends of each pin, before being covered by blood, embossed with the silhouette of a wolf.

She presses down on his shoulders as his body jerks, quavers, shudders. He is still inside her, and she moans with the pleasure from his movements, even as his hands try, and fail, to get at her hands, to get at his neck.

She stands, dripping and wet, pours herself some wine, turns to address the bed.

"A man who thinks he's a wolf still dies like a dog," the wolf says, as she raises her glass, swirling the wine within; deeply, darkly–

Red.

The Siren and the Sailor

The sailor knows, as all sailors know, of the sirens.

He knows they live upon an isle, that their song compelled men, that ships would crash upon the rocks, and thus and there the men would die.

He knows King Odysseus of Ithaca, alone amongst men, had heard their song and lived.

Upon these two facts all men could agree.

And thus the legends go–

That they were the daughters of Melpomene, herself the daughter of Mnemosyne, herself the daughter of Earth and Sky.

That they were the companions of Persephone, given wings by Demeter.

That their song is so beautiful as to drive men mad with passion, wherein those men could think of nothing but to sate themselves upon the singer.

That their song promised knowledge and the power which comes with it, wherein even the wise would find things worth learning, the very secrets cherished and held by the Gods Themselves.

Thus the legends go.

In all these tales, the sailor could find no answer to the one question he had.

As a sailor, he collected the tales of the sirens, and he could find his answer in none of them.

As a captain, his hobby flowered into obsession, for he could not find his answer in all of them.

As a merchant, with many a ship for him to direct, he possesses wealth beyond the imagining of a simple sailor, but there is none from whom he could purchase his answer.

Finally, he realises the only way forwards, the only way he could be at peace, is to seek out a siren, and ask of her his question.

So be it, the sailor thinks, and he walks into the hallowed halls of the temple to Apollo, God of Music. Before that great marble statue, he swears, he swears with all his heart and all his faith he would devote both time and treasure to the seeking of his answer, and he begged, he begged with all his heart and all his faith for the blessing of Apollo, who was also God of Truth.

Thus he prepares.

If their song would drive men mad with passion, then he needs be free of passion. So he squanders his wealth on the most beautiful women money could rent. He does this until there is no woman, however alluring her form, however clever her wit, who could still retain his interest, and so he rids himself of all the promises of the flesh.

If their song would promise wisdom and truth, then, well, good. For he had but one question.

To survive the passage to their isle, he finds himself an artificer, brilliant and cunning, apprentice, it is said, to an apprentice of Daedalus himself. The artificer crafts for him a boat of bronze, which surprises and delights the sailor with the power of its magics, for upon the waters the boat would not sink, though it be made of metal. Upon the crashing rocks it would not sink, for it be made of metal.

Thus prepared, the sailor set sail for the isle of the sirens, a passenger upon the very ship he had once been so proud a captain of.

The crew, men grown tough between the blazing sun and the shining sea, cry without shame the tears of their frustration, for they could not dissuade him from what all knew would be certain death. He has gone mad, but he is still their captain, and they still hold him in such vaulted esteem it may be called "love".

Still he has his question, and, still, he has to have his answer.

Thus his metal boat is lowered into the waters. Far as to be almost upon the horizon lies the isle of the sirens, where the song and the answer beckoned.

Behind him, as he sailed, the ship that he loves waits and watches.

And thus he hears the song, softly at first, like the whispering of the wind, and he brings out his paddles, and starts to row.

And thus he hears the song, light as the breeze and full and filled with exquisite beauty, and he rows harder.

And so it goes.

His bronze boat *dings* and *dangs* as the rocks assault it, but it does not break, it does not sink. Amongst rotting wood and bleached bones, it sails, for it does not break, it does not sink.

And, finally, the song loud and clear in his head and in his heart, he finds himself ashore, standing upon sand no mortal man has ever stood upon.

The sailor follows the song, certain it is to be his dirge, until he finds himself in a lush meadow, and there, before him, is a young woman, white feathery wings folded upon her back.

She is singing, bent over as she picks flowers. She is exquisite, and she is beautiful. She is the flame of which her song is the light. She is the flame of which men turn moth to embrace and die.

He nears her and she looks up. She drops her flowers in her shock.

But still she sings, the melody soaring out of her becoming urgent.

She withdraws as he walks towards her, pushed back by the crazed madness of his eyes.

But still she sings.

She stumbles as she steps backwards, alarmed by the clenching of his fist.

But still she sings.

And then she stops singing.

Because he has punched her in the throat.

Finally, the answer he has devoted his life to lay before him, with terrified eyes upon the ground, one hand around the pain in her throat, one hand raised to ward him off.

The answer.

"People die when you sing," he shouts at her. "You must know that! So tell me! Just tell me! Why don't you just shut the fuck up?"

The Lake and the Moon

"Water falls," she says.

It was a childish prank, played by a child.

Next to the road to the capital, the mirrored water of the lake reflects the light of the crescent moon. The wind gently blows, ripples and waves lapping upon the shore.

Upon that shore, a tea house sits, weathered wood offering shelter and food to the travellers going to and away from the capital. There is a bustle here, at this hour, after evening has faded to night, before bones become too weary for companionship.

As the capital is the heart of the world, the tea house is the heart of the village, and it is here the men come, after the fishing is done, the wood is gathered, the hunting is over.

Here then, here, at the edge of the light and the laughter of the tea house, upon the shore with the lapping waves, a small girl stands crying.

It was a childish prank, played by a child.

One side of the tea house is built over the lake. The fish, still alive, caught earlier in the day would be lowered in cages; each wooden cell opened by the lifting of a knob, thereby lifting the side of the cage attached to that knob.

An order would come for a fish – broiled or fried or steamed – and the cook's assistant would pull out one of the cages, carry it away from the lake, place it upon the ground, lift up the wall of the cage, then, with practised hand, grab hold of the struggling, threshing fish, beat its head against the floor, just the once.

The cook's assistant had found the child, lying flat upon the floor, her face pressed against the rails overlooking the lake. He had walked to the rails to look over them and he had seen the long stick she held in her outstretched hand, seen where the wood split at the end of her stick as she lifted it out of the water. He had yelled out. He had pulled her up by the scruff of her neck.

Her mother had come, deeply unhappy, her face drawn with the scowl of exhausted displeasure. "Not again," the scowl said. "Stay here till your father comes to pick you up," the disapproving voice said. "I am sick of having to deal with your nonsense," the undercurrent of the disapproving voice said.

It was a childish prank, played by a child.

Now, right now, her father is in there, as she stands looking at the lapping waters. Her father had come, an hour ago, had done no more than look at her, shake his head. She had glanced at him, plaintive and pleading; "I'm sorry," her eyes had said, "take me away." She had watched him apologise to the cook. The cook had been angry, then not-angry, then, perhaps, a little sad, a flow of emotion drawn out from an emotionless man by the snivelling apology of her father. The cook had guided her father to a table, brought him a drink, patted him on the shoulder. The cook had looked at her, shook his head. Her father sits there now, looking out at the waters, not looking at her.

It was a childish prank, played by a child.

The maiden tells this story to the man she had first met just this night, beneath the gaze of the crescent moon.

She stands at the spot just on the edge of the light and life of the tea house, on the shore of the lake, looking out upon the waters, on this, a night like the night in the story.

The man had come, had stood by her, had seen the same scene she saw; but the lake did not mean the same thing to the man as it did to the maiden.

It starts with small talk, presumably, because that's what strangers do. But the hours had passed and he had not left, and neither had she, and they had gone from standing to sitting upon the hard earth, and then she is telling him the story of how she had witnessed a small girl let the fishes go. "It was a childish prank, played by a child."

"But not to the child."

She turns to him; he is looking out upon the waters, upon the sliver of the moon upon the rippling waves. "What makes you say that?"

"The stick."

"..."

"You make it sound like this is the act of a playful child, whose parents are frustrated with her. A childish prank, you say. But it is not simple to find a stick long enough, with a fork at the end, in order to hook the knob to open the cage."

"You think she thought it through? That she planned it?"

"How could she not? How could it be random whimsy? She went out and she found a stick so she could go and rescue the fish."

The maiden turns back to the waters, and they sit there, in silence. She thinks about how she had told this story before, to a few others, though not many, yet no one else had thought it to be anything more than the prank she said it was.

And then she says: "I am to marry a man next month. A weak, feckless man."

He turns to her; she is looking out upon the waters. Her eyes, perhaps, are shiny, reflecting the moon as the lake does.

She shakes her head. "I don't know why I said that."

She points to the sliver of the moon in the centre of the lake. "The water is still. And the moon in the lake is as the moon in the sky. The wind comes, and the reflection ripples, and the moon in the lake is revealed to be no more than a false moon. But the moon, the moon itself, it does not know, it does not care."

"Is that what you see? Falsehood? An uncaring light over an uncaring world?"

"What else is there to see? Like the girl. She saves five fish, but the day after, and the day after that, more fish are caught. For a moment, she made the world better, but the wind comes, and that better world is revealed as a lie. The moon merely looks on; we cannot catch it, we cannot change it. For a brief moment, we can be like the moon, but only until the wind comes. You cannot save all the fish."

He turns to look at her, the maiden with her shiny eyes. "You cannot save all the fish. But you can save one. I am sure there are other stories about the lake and the moon."

"Tell me the story."

But the man doesn't know any stories.

The mother tells this story to her young son.

They stand at the spot just on the edge of the light and life of the tea house, on the shore of the lake, looking out upon the waters, on this, a night like the night in the story, and in the story within that story.

"I know the man's story."

His mother laughs. "Do you?"

"Yes," the boy says, all seriousness, as children can be.

"Tell me the story."

"You didn't say 'please'."

"Please tell me the story, little man."

He nods with solemnity, then he begins, his voice taking on the cadence of one reciting from memory: "Once there was a fish who had been caught. There was a kind girl who let the fish go. The fish was very grateful for this and decided it had to repay the girl, but it was only a fish.

"So the fish swam and swam, it swam from the lake into the river, from river into the sea, until it came to the palace of the Dragon of the Eastern Sea. It asked of the Dragon, who was old and wise, how could a simple fish repay the great debt it owed. The Dragon told the fish it had to swim to a waterfall and at the top of the waterfall the fish would find its answer.

"The fish swam and swam, it swam back to the lake, up the river, swam till it reached the waterfall. The fish swam up the waterfall. But, because it was only a fish, and fishes are not meant to swim up waterfalls, it fell back into the river, and it was swept away until it reached the lake.

"The fish kept trying. Night after night, as the moon changes from crescent to full and back again, the fish kept trying. It grew bigger, and stronger, through the seasons, through the years. It waits until the moon is above the waterfall, and it keeps the light of the moon in its sight as it swims, trying always, to swim up the waterfall to the light of the moon.

"And then one night, after years and years of never giving up, it finally swarm up the bridge across the sky. The fish gained magic powers, and this was how it managed to repay the girl who had given it back its life."

"How do you know this story?"

"Daddy tells it to me, sometimes, when it's his turn to put me in bed."

"He never told me this story."

"You can ask him to. He calls it the story of How a Fish Swam Up a Waterfall to Fall for a Girl."

The young man tells this story to the pretty girl.

They stand at the spot just on the edge of the light and life of the tea house, on the shore of the lake, looking out upon the waters, on this, a night like the night in the story, and in the stories within that story.

"And that is why our tea house on the lake does not serve fish."

The pretty girl curls her fingers into his, drops her head upon his shoulder. "She rescues a fish, and the fish rescues her?"

"Pretty much. A childish prank, played by a child."

"But not to the girl."

"But not to the fish."

About the Author

CHESTER TANYEO, author, philosopher-poet and cult leader (part-time), wrote the Witch-Girl series, short story collections, *The Bridge Across the Sky* and *The Lingering Solitude of the Girl on the Moon (and Other Single-Serving Stories)*, and *The Glass-Like Girl (And Other Rhymes)*.

Chester likes long titles and cats.

http://nocturne.noctalis.com
http://facebook.com/chestertanyeo
http://patreon.com/noctalis